MEAD
PUBLIC LIBRARY

In memory of
Charles E. Carroll

Donated by family
and friends

2010

SAMURAI KIDS

WHITE CRANE

SAMURAI KIDS

WHITE CRANE

SANDY FUSSELL

CANDLEWICK PRESS

Text copyright © 2010 by Sandy Fussell
Illustrations copyright © 2010 by Rhian Nest James

First U.S. edition 2010

Library of Congress Cataloging-in-Publication Data

Fussell, Sandy.
White crane / by Sandy Fussell ; illustrated by Rhian Nest James. — 1st ed.
      p.   cm. — (Samurai kids)
      Summary: Even though he has only one leg, Niya Moto is
      studying to be a samurai, and his five fellow-students are
    similarly burdened, but sensei Ki-Yaga, an ancient but legendary
    warrior, teaches them not only physical skills but mental and
    spiritual ones as well, so that they are well-equipped to face their
      most formidable opponents at the annual Samurai Games.
                 ISBN 978-0-7636-4503-8
    [1. Samurai — Fiction. 2. People with disabilities — Fiction.
3. Contests — Fiction. 4. Schools — Fiction. 5. Japan — Fiction.]
      I. James, Rhian Nest, date– ill. II. Title. III. Series.
                 PZ7.F96669Wh 2010
                 [Fic] — dc22   2009037863

10 11 12 13 14 15 BVG 10 9 8 7 6 5 4 3 2 1

Printed in Berryville, VA, U.S.A.

This book was typset in Garamond Three.

Candlewick Press
99 Dover Street
Somerville, Massachusetts 02144

visit us at www.candlewick.com

For Jackson, who opened the door
S. F.

For Elis
R. N. J.

THE SAMURAI KIDS

KYOKO A white-haired girl with pink eyes and extra fingers and toes. Her spirit is the Snow Monkey.

MIKKO A one-armed boy. His spirit is the Striped Gecko.

NIYA The one-legged boy who narrates
the story. His spirit is the White Crane.

YOSHI A huge, strong boy who doesn't
want to fight. He doesn't know
what his spirit is.

TAJI A blind boy. His spirit is the Golden Bat.

THE TEACHER

SENSEI Also known as Ki-Yaga the wizard. He was once a famous samurai warrior.

CONTENTS

CHAPTER ONE

真

LITTLE
COCKROACHES

"Aye-eee-yah!"

I scissor-kick as high as I can and land on my right foot. I haven't got another one. My name is Niya Moto, and I'm the only one-legged samurai kid in Japan. Usually I miss my foot and land on my backside. Or flat on my face in the dirt.

I'm not good at exercises, but I'm great at standing on one leg. Raising my arms over my head, I pretend I am the White Crane. "Look at me!" the crane screeches across the training ground. "Look at him," the valley echoes.

But Sensei Ki-Yaga is not looking. My master sits in the sun with his back against the old, stooped cherry tree. He is as ancient as the mountains around our school and as dilapidated as the equipment we use. Most people think he died years ago.

2

Eyes shut, he's not watching me practice. That lazy old man slept through the only upright landing I've ever made! I lower my right arm, and the White Crane makes a rude gesture with its wing.

Sensei's wrinkled mouth creaks into a smile, but his eyes stay hidden behind closed lids. "A boy who cannot perfectly execute even half a scissor-kick should not waste time finding fault with his teacher. More practice, Little Cockroach." His voice rumbles like thunder.

"Yes, Master." I bow low to show my respect. Even though he is strict, I like Sensei, and I never forget that he was the only teacher not bothered by my missing leg.

"I am not a counter of feet," he told me. "I am a collector of more important parts. And when I buy you socks, they will last twice as long."

When the Cockroach Ryu wrote and offered me a samurai traineeship, Father was impressed.

"Look, Niya. Master Ki-Yaga wielded a sword in the days of legend, when the samurai were great and powerful. They fought in real battles then, not tournament rings like today."

"I thought he was dead," Mother added.

"So did I. He must be extremely old, but not too frail to write and ask for our boy."

Mother and Father are pushovers for a famous name, even an almost dead one. They looked at me proudly, as if I had done something special. I stood straight and tall on my one leg, and pretended I had. Anything, if they would let me go.

"It's too far away," Mother finally said. "The Cockroach Ryu is in the Tateyama Mountains. It's too cold there."

In the end the decision made itself. I had no other offers. Even my father's old school, the Dragon Ryu, would not take me. "We regret to inform you we cannot accept a one-legged boy," their letter said. Father went to see the Dragon people, to yell they were honor-bound to teach his son, but they wouldn't even answer him.

"The Dragon Ryu is not good enough for Niya," Father announced. "Niya will go to Ki-Yaga."

I wondered why such a great man wanted to teach a crippled boy. Maybe he felt sorry for me. But I didn't care. I desperately wanted to be a samurai. I would've hopped all the way to the mountains if necessary.

"Grandfather!" I called out to my elder who shared

4

our house. "Grandfather, I am to study with Sensei Ki-Yaga."

"I thought he was dead," Grandfather answered.

Three years have passed since the day of the letter. My town life is long gone. I am fourteen now, and this old school high on the mountain is my home. For another three years I will study here, and when I leave, I'll be a samurai warrior.

"Yah! Yah-ah!"

I punch the air with my foot and land on the other one I haven't got. Sprawled out on the grass, I lift my face to see if Sensei is watching this time. Even though his lids are still closed, the wrinkles at the edge of his face are smiling.

My bamboo crutch lies useless beside him. He won't let me use it when I practice.

"You don't need that," he says. "It will weigh you down."

Now, with my mouth full of dirt, I think I need some extra weight for balance. But I never give up, because in my heart I am the White Crane, proud and defiant.

When I was too young to carry a sword, Father took

me to a lake to fish. A tall, thin bird stood at the water's edge.

Staring at me with shining black eyes, the crane slowly tucked one leg up under its body. One-legged, just like me! My spirit totem flew into my heart. When I look into the mirror, I don't see my reflection; I see the White Crane. If I am afraid, it crouches with me and I'm not alone. When I am happy, it screeches my gladness to the world.

"More practice, Little Cockroach," Sensei growls.

Lifting itself out of the grime, the White Crane shakes the dust from its snowy feathers.

"Eee-yah!" it cries as I begin the move again.

On the same day that I arrived at the Cockroach Ryu, three boys and one girl also came to the school's old, empty rooms: Mikko, with his one arm; Yoshi, who is huge and strong, but refuses to fight; Kyoko, who has an extra finger and an extra toe, and is a girl; Taji, blind in both eyes. And me. We're the unwanted. Unwanted everywhere else but here.

"A cracked bowl can hold water. There is nothing

wrong with the bowl. It just needs to be held properly,"
Sensei instructs.

"Huh?" says Mikko.

Mikko's brain doesn't like to think unless it has to.

"He means we are just as capable as everyone else.
Maybe even better, with the right teacher," says Taji.
Taji thinks a lot, because he can't see. He likes to sit in
the sun and meditate. Sensei sits beside Taji with his
eyes closed so he can't see either. Their *oms* drift through
the practice ground. Closing my eyes, I think of Taji,
who has two legs but has never seen the practice ring.

"Oy. Aye-yah. Oy!" I cry.

I kick high and land solid on my foot. Perfectly.
Hopping around in excitement, the White Crane
dances on one leg.

"Well done," Sensei calls.

Taji joins our teacher in the sun. "Great landing, Ni."

"How did you know?" I ask Taji later at dinner.

"There is nothing wrong with my ears," he retorts.
"I am used to the sounds of you hitting the dirt. Face-
first: *Splat!* Butt-first: *Phlat!* This was a new sound.

"Oy. Aye-yah. Oy!" I cry.

One I've never heard before." He laughs at me, but it doesn't hurt the way it does when others laugh.

"Attention!" Sensei bangs the big drum beside his table. It means put down your chopsticks and listen. Put them down fast or he'll crack you over the knuckles.

"The Annual Samurai Trainee Games begin soon. This year, we will again contest the team event. We must work hard." Sensei bangs the drum to indicate that we can resume eating.

My appetite is gone.

"I hate the Games," I say.

"I'm sick of coming last," moans Kyoko.

Mikko bashes his one fist on the table. "I'm tired of being laughed at by the Dragons."

"And the Eagles. And everyone else," I add. I can still hear the taunts: 'Look at the frog hop.' I'd like to see them fight with one leg bound up or one arm tied behind their back.

"Why do we have to be the Cockroach Ryu? Why must we have such a wretched name?" Yoshi is big, and his voice booms even when he whispers.

"Cockroach is a strong, powerful name," says Sensei.

Kyoko laughs out loud. She can get away with it because she is a girl and has Sensei wrapped around her extra finger. The rest of us are laughing inside. But Sensei knows; he knows everything inside or out.

"I will tell you a story. Bring your dessert bowls to the mat and you may eat while I talk," he says.

Sensei's tales are magical. Our eyes shine with the expectation of honey rice pudding and a story.

Sensei tucks his feet underneath his body. Now he is less than me. No legs. Looking at me, he smiles. Then he tucks both arms behind his back and closes his eyes. He is one of us.

"Ever since the beginning, the cockroach has been mightier than the dragon. If a dragon stands between a boy and his honey pudding, the boy will challenge the dragon. The boy will fight, and sometimes he will win. Sometimes he will die. He doesn't care. A samurai boy will take great risks and fight hard for pudding."

We all nod. It's true. There's no finer food in the whole of Japan.

"The cockroach is mightier than the dragon." Sensei

raises his arms dramatically and shakes his long sleeves toward us. Cockroaches pour into our plates.

"Yuck!" screams Kyoko.

Looking at my pudding in dismay, I see one cockroach swimming laps and another waving its bottom in my face.

"Eat up," says Sensei, lifting his bowl.

Taji shakes his head.

"See?" Ki-Yaga laughs. "The cockroach is mightier than the dragon. A boy will throw out his pudding if a cockroach has stepped in it. He will not even try to fight."

Sensei stands up and walks back to the table. There is nothing wrong with his dessert. Slurping honey pudding, he studies our faces to see if we understand. Then he folds his long white beard under his kimono sash and closes his eyes to sleep.

My friends and I take our bowls outside. We've learned the lesson, all right. Next time Sensei tells a story, cover up your food.

"One, two, three," Yoshi counts.

We swish our bowls skyward. Cockroaches and honey pudding rain over the grass.

CHAPTER TWO

BAD BREATH
AND BIG FEET

One of the best things about being a samurai kid is that you get a sword. A really sharp one. When I was five, Father gave me my first blade.

"Come here, Niya," he called, his voice gruff and shaking. I thought he was crying and ran quickly because I didn't want him to be sad.

But he wasn't sad. He was smiling. On his lap was a long bundle of red silk tied with string.

"This was mine, and now it's yours," he said, unwrapping the sword to show me the White Crane carved on its handle. Nicks and scratches flecked the shiny blade, but I didn't care. I loved it as soon as I saw it.

My heart swelled, and the White Crane spread its new wings. My one leg didn't matter when the crane flew high above the ground.

"I am proud of you." Blowing his nose and dabbing

at his eyes with his handkerchief, Father tucked his old sword in my sash belt.

"Don't chase your sister with it," he said.

I am much older now, but I still carry the sword with me every day. A samurai's sword is part of his body. I named the blade Izuru, and it is my best friend. Along with Mikko, Taji, Yoshi, and Kyoko.

When we practice sword fighting, we use wooden sticks. We're not allowed to use real swords. In the Dragon Ryu, they fight with real swords, but with no honor. They even cheat against each other. That's how Mikko lost his arm, when he was a student there.

Sensei says that a true swordsman doesn't need a blade.

"The point of the sword is . . ." Sensei pauses mid-sentence to make sure we are all paying attention.

I know this one. The point of the sword is to defend with dignity.

"The point of the sword is very sharp," Sensei says.

That's true, too.

This morning my opponent is Mikko. You'd think it would be easy to fight a one-armed kid. It's not. Mikko is an ace swordsman who could fight with no arms and a blade between his teeth. Those Dragon kids would never have beaten him if it wasn't three against one.

"Hey, you've got to tie your arm behind your back," Mikko says.

It's the rules. Sensei says you have to be able to fight on your opponent's terms.

I fold an arm behind my back.

"Not that one. The other one. Same as me."

"Come on, Mikko," I complain. "I'm right-handed. It's not fair to make me fight left-handed."

He grins. "I fight left-handed."

"You were *born* left-handed."

"It's the rules." He won't give in.

"You have to tie your leg up then," I insist.

Snoring under the cherry tree, Sensei listens in his sleep. Sensei teaches us Bushido. It's the samurai code, all about rules. Lots of rules. Do what is right. Be honorable. Be polite. Duty first.

"And always obey your teacher," Sensei's voice cuts through my thoughts. Sometimes I think Ki-Yaga is a wizard, not a warrior master. With blue demon eyes, he reaches inside our heads when we are not looking.

Learning Bushido is not difficult. All we have to do is listen, and Sensei is a wonderful storyteller. Calligraphy, our next lesson, is hard work. Such a waste of time! Hours of boring brushwork and smudged ink. No one can ever read anything I write anyway.

I much prefer the practice field. But it's not enough to be good with a sword; a samurai has to have neat handwriting, too. There's even a calligraphy event at the Samurai Trainee Games.

"I hate calligraphy class," I groan.

"You shouldn't whine," complains Mikko. "It's hard with one hand."

"You don't need two hands to write."

"I do. You should try it with just one hand," he says.

"What about me?" Kyoko grins. "The brush is too short for my extra finger."

"That's nothing. What about me? I can't even see the page." Blind Taji laughs at himself, and everyone chimes in. Yoshi's deep guffaws wake our snoring teacher.

"More practice, Little Cockroaches," Sensei interrupts. "I do not have all day to spend sleeping in the sun. *Chi! Jin! Yu!*"

Wisdom, benevolence, and courage. The code of the samurai.

"*Chi!*" I yell and wave my wooden stick.

"*Jin!*" Mikko brandishes his in return.

"*Yu!*"

We charge toward each other. Mikko, the expert swordsman, forgets he has one leg tied up and falls flat on his face.

"Ni wins," Kyoko announces as I help Mikko to his feet.

"The Striped Gecko will get you next time," Mikko taunts me with his spirit totem.

I wave my pole and do a victory hopping dance. "I'm not scared. The White Crane is not afraid of little lizards. I eat geckos for breakfast."

Later we sit in origami class.

"Watch this," Kyoko says.

With fingers twisting and twirling, she spins a light brown square of paper until it becomes an old man with scrawny arms and weedy legs. Sometimes it helps to have an extra finger.

"It's Sensei," she says, giggling.

Kyoko is not like my sister. My sister wears cherry blossom kimonos and smells like flowers. Kyoko is one of us. She smells like sweat and kicks hard. Her hair is rice white, and her eyes are pale pink.

"Freak girl," the kids from the other *ryu* jeer.

I don't think she's a freak. When she laughs and shakes her head, I think of falling snow.

"What's this?" Sensei appears beside me.

Ki-Yaga looks like a fragile paper man. Tall and gaunt, old skin stretched over ancient bones. But those skinny arms are strong and the bones unbreakable. I saw him pick Taji up one-handed when Taji tripped during training, and once he placed his finger against my neck and I couldn't move a muscle.

"Beautiful work, Kyoko," Sensei says. "Such a skinny old man. He looks like my grandfather. Now, my Little Cockroaches, make something from your heart."

I make the White Crane. It's an easy exercise, even for my clumsy fingers. Soon the White Crane, the Snow Monkey, the Striped Gecko, and the Golden Bat stand together on the table. Our spirit totems are always with us. Even in origami lessons.

Only Yoshi doesn't make anything, because he hasn't found his totem yet. It must be hard not to have one. I can't remember a time when the White Crane wasn't part of me.

"What about you, Yoshi?" Taji asks. Even without eyes, he knows we are one spirit short.

Yoshi shakes his head. "I don't feel like it."

"Is that why you don't fight?" asks Kyoko.

"Yes," he whispers. "I don't feel like it."

It's suddenly quiet. We wait for Yoshi to keep talking, to tell us why. But he doesn't. He looks at Sensei, who says nothing, too.

Our team would be much stronger if Yoshi wrestled and swung his sword for us. He's twice as big as me and as strong as a bear.

Pop! Kyoko squashes a paper box of air to break the silence.

"I bet the Dragons aren't wasting time playing with paper," mutters Mikko.

Kyoko's fingers fly again, and a dragon breathes along the tabletop.

"Whoosh." She blows hard, and our origami animals

topple over. The White Crane lies on its back, legs in the air.

Sensei takes his place at the head of the table. "The Dragon's breath is nothing but hot air. And it smells like dead goldfish," he says.

"I'm more worried about the Dragon's feet," admits Taji. "Cockroaches can get stomped."

Closing his eyes, Sensei rocks from side to side.

A story is coming. The White Crane folds its wings to listen.

"This is the last Dragon story I will tell you. Listen and you will never be afraid again. Many years ago, in the early mists of the mountain, the dragon Ryujin went walking. A dragon has scales of steel, but its feet are soft. It trod on a thorn. The great creature roared in pain. Huge claws could not remove something so small.

"Wind carried Ryujin's cries deep into the earth, but the other animals closed their ears. No one wanted to help the cruel, boastful dragon. Only Gokiburi, the cockroach, came to help. The cockroach was kind and wise.

"'I will help you because no creature is so great it stands alone. Even a proud dragon must sometimes bend before a cockroach,' it said.

"The dragon bowed, and the cockroach removed the thorn. So you see, Little Cockroaches, when the time comes, you will find power over the dragon. Bad breath and big feet are not to be feared."

Taking the last square of paper, Sensei folds a cockroach. It's very difficult. Even Kyoko can't do it.

"More practice! Train hard!" Sensei strides from the room.

Taji grins. "I bet they don't tell that story at the Dragon Ryu."

"I'd love to beat them, just once," says Yoshi. "Even if it was only at calligraphy. Or origami."

"We can do it at sword fighting! I know we can. Let's go practice." Mikko waves his weapon in the air.

I'm not so sure we can win, but I'm going to try harder than ever.

In the training ring, it's Taji's turn to fight me. Taji bends his leg up. Yoshi places a blindfold over my eyes.

I leap forward. I can't find Taji anywhere.

All I can see is blue silk. All I can hear is my friends' playful laughter.

Around and around we circle, poking and stabbing at air. I leap forward. I can't find Taji anywhere. Taji's skilled ears have no trouble tracking my clumsy moves, but it doesn't matter if he knows where I am or not. He can't reach me from where he has fallen rump first in the dirt.

"No one wins," announces Kyoko.

The ground shakes. *Thump! Thump! Thump!* We all land in the dust. The Tateyama are fire-breathing mountains.

"The dragon laughs at us," says Mikko, looking up as if he expects fire and ash to rain down.

I sneak a look, too. Just in case he's right.

"No. The dragon is afraid," Sensei instructs from under the cherry tree. "When I was first old, the mountain erupted with fire. Many people thought I was dead."

They still do, I think with a smile.

Sensei looks at me, and his too-bright blue eyes sparkle in the sun. "Cockroaches are small, but they are very hard to kill," he says.

CHAPTER THREE

名誉

EGG ROLL

Boom, boom! The sound of Sensei's drum echoes into the valley. It reaches every corner of the *ryu* and crashes into the garden where Yoshi, Mikko, Kyoko, and I are planting *dokudami* herb. We work quickly, with clothespins on our noses. *Dokudami* stinks like rotten fish heads.

Sensei uses the herb to make medicinal wine, which he trades for supplies at the village in the valley.

"Magic always smells fishy in the noses of men," our wizard master says, inhaling from the bottle.

Sensei's thin hooked nose is filled with thick noodle balls of white nostril hair. The smell doesn't bother him at all!

Once, when I ate so much honey pudding my stomach wanted to explode, Sensei gave me a small glass of his wine. *Ye-ech!* I didn't even need to drink it. One fish-laden sniff and I forgot I had a stomach.

Taji isn't gardening. Even though he can't see, he's chasing chickens to sharpen his wrestling reflexes. *Cluck-tuk!* The terrified chicken dodges sideways. Taji dives toward the sound but misses and skids face-first through a row of cabbages.

"You didn't catch the chicken, but you scared it egg-less." Yoshi picks up a warm new egg.

Kyoko giggles. "Well done. You caught an egg instead of a chicken." She takes the egg from Yoshi and puts it in her pocket.

Boom, boom, the drum insists. We run to see what our master wants.

Sensei waits, dozing cross-legged beneath the cherry tree. The drum and two traveling hats rest in his lap. When a samurai goes into a village or town, he wears a big, wide bamboo hat to cover his face.

"Why does the samurai hide his face?" Mikko asked the first time Sensei showed us the hats.

"It is tradition to hide the face, in case of accidental dishonor. Or rain. A samurai does not like to be embarrassed, and he hates to get wet."

It makes good sense to me. There's nothing worse

than a soggy kimono lapping at your ankles. And the village is a busy, confusing place where anything could happen. It's full of strange things and something we rarely see — other kids. Samurai training *ryu* regularly visit each other to play friendly tournaments. But not us. Sensei says no.

"Why can't we travel to another *ryu*?" I ask.

"There is nothing to learn there, and I have already taught you nothing."

"Couldn't we visit the Mountain Eagles? It's not very far," Taji cajoles. The Mountain Eagle Ryu is closest to us, on the other side of Mount Tateyama. Eagle trainees are famous for their flying acrobatic kicks.

Sensei shakes his head. "Sparrows. Puny birdseed eaters."

"What about the Snakes?" asks Mikko. "They're strong wrestlers and eat raw meat."

"Wriggling worms. Raw meat makes smelly droppings." Sensei wrinkles his nose.

They couldn't smell worse than *dokudami* in the morning sun. But in Sensei's closed eyes, no one is good enough for the mighty Cockroaches. Still, I wish we could practice against normal kids. Just sometimes.

The wizard Ki-Yaga reads my mind. "What is normal?" he asks.

It's a Zen question. Sensei is a Zen Master and teaches us to study questions so we can become wise samurai. The hardest question is: "What is the sound of one hand clapping?"

Mikko knows the answer to that one. Clapping with one hand is what a one-armed kid does all the time.

Zen questions are easy for me because I know the secret. It's NOTHING. The answer to every question is some sort of NOTHING. If you say nothing, you are wise because you already know the answer and don't need to speak it. If you jump up and yell NOTHING, you are wise and generous with your knowledge.

This morning I feel noisy, generous, and wise. I know what is normal.

"NOTHING!" I shout.

"Very good, Niya. Now, sit down and listen," Sensei instructs.

We sit in a half circle, and I try to concentrate. It's not a story this time. The White Crane's head droops in the heat, but Sensei's stern glance snaps it upright.

"I have ordered many things in the village, and they need to be collected today," he says.

Crossing my fingers, I hope I can go. Every month two of us trek partway down the mountain path to pick up supplies the villagers leave on the big, flat halfway rock, but we rarely go all the way to the village.

The White Crane crosses its clawed feet while I hold my breath.

"Yoshi will go because he is strong and there is much to carry. Niya will go because he is quick to calculate and remembers everything I tell him."

Aaa-aah. I can breathe again. My master doesn't look at weaknesses, only strengths. One leg and a clumsy crutch don't matter. I am going because my mind can outrun other two-legged brains.

"Rice cakes, arrowheads, string, wrestling oil, dried fish . . ." Sensei recites a list of things I have to remember, provisions for our journey to the Trainee Games. As each item is named, I catch it with my mind. When there are no more words, Sensei hands Yoshi a big harness for strapping packages to his back. Three bottles of *dokudami* wine are tied to the frame. Thick stoppers hold the liquid and its smell in place.

"Last, you will visit Onaku, the Sword Master. He has a message for me."

My heart jumps high. The Sword Master is crafting our new swords! In four days, at our Coming-of-Age Ceremony, we swap our childhood weapons for the *katana* and the *wakizashi:* the long, curved blade and the short, sharp dagger of a warrior samurai. Our studying will be half over.

The White Crane strains to fly skyward.

Yoshi puts on a traveling hat, tilting it forward to cover his face. I do the same.

"Be careful you don't trip." Taji laughs. "Now, if it were me, I don't need to see where I'm going. . . ."

Sensei puts his fingers to his lips. No more talking.

"Go quickly, Little Cockroaches. You must scurry to the village before sunset. The path grows treacherous."

Everyone looks surprised.

31

"The path was never dangerous before." Mikko voices our thoughts.

"What was true yesterday might be a lie today. Paths always change," says Sensei.

"Perhaps they shouldn't go." Kyoko worriedly fiddles with the egg in her pocket.

"A samurai runs toward danger." Sensei raises his arms. "Hurry! Hurry!"

It is our signal to leave.

With Sensei's warning stalking our heels, we hasten downward. The path is steep and narrows in places where we have to hug the mountainside as we edge around the rocky outcrops. Even with my crutch under my arm, I am a fast walker and have no trouble keeping up with Yoshi's long strides. It's a four-hour walk to the village, so we'll be there long before sunset.

"I can't see anything different. There's no danger here," I say. The White Crane swoops out into the valley, and my heart is as light as its feathers.

"I don't think there is anything to worry about. Sensei probably has a lesson hidden somewhere," agrees Yoshi.

Sensei never stops teaching. "Life is a lesson," he says. I wish the lessons were more interesting. Like how many bowls of honey rice pudding can a boy eat in five minutes? Or how far can an egg roll?

But Sensei asks difficult questions. Questions like: "Which came first: the chicken or the egg?"

I like to think with my stomach. The egg came first because it's omelette for breakfast and chicken noodles for dinner.

The question reminds me of the lunch Sensei packed. "I'm hungry."

Yoshi's stomach growls. "Me too."

Unwrapping little parcels of egg and chicken rice, I wonder if maybe the chicken and the egg came together.

We eat and walk. Since we left the *ryu,* I haven't seen a single living thing. Not even a bird. While I search the sky, a lizard darts across under my feet, forcing me to lurch forward. Strong arms steady me. Yoshi has a wrestler's timing. I want to say, "If you fight for us, we're sure to win the wrestling event." But we try not to ask Yoshi why he doesn't want to fight. "Thanks," I say instead.

I feel better now that I have seen a lizard. It reminds me of Mikko. Poor Striped Gecko stuck in the classroom practicing calligraphy, while Yoshi and I munch our way down the mountain.

"Maybe the Games won't be so bad this year," I mumble through a mouthful.

"I think we will surprise people," says Yoshi.

That's for sure. The sight of us — one-armed, one-legged, and the rest — is a surprise every time.

Yoshi's mood matches mine. Happy. Excited. We kick stones over the edge.

Farther along the track, a flock of pitta birds flies upward. Another group follows. Their bright red, blue, and green wings swamp the sky with feathers. The air echoes with their frightened *piphy-piphy* calls. Then nothing. It's suddenly still and silent.

"Eerie," murmurs Yoshi.

The White Crane agrees. It wants to open its wings and follow the pitta birds.

As a cloud moves over the sun, the mountain grows cold and gray. There's nothing strange about that. Mountain and Sun argue all the time, and the sun often sulks behind a cloud. Sensei's warning clangs inside my head. If the sun doesn't return, it might be dark before we reach the village. We need to hurry.

I recite Sensei's list aloud to make sure I don't forget anything. And to keep myself from thinking about frightened birds and shadows and mountain goblins and—

"Shh," Yoshi interrupts, pointing up the ridge. The silhouette of a huge gray wolf lopes along the path above us. My heart hiccups. No one has ever seen a wolf on this mountain. Old people say the wolf uses magical powers to transform into a man. While I watch, the wolf sniffs the air, then disappears into nothing.

Thickening gloom reminds me of Sensei's soup and the tales my grandfather tells.

"The gray wolf is a shape-shifter." Grandfather

The animals know, and I can feel it.

rolled his eyes as he told the story, and my stomach somersaulted nervously. "One day a samurai came upon a gray wolf, and when it attacked him, he cut it across the leg. The wolf ran away. Then another wolf attacked him, and he cut its neck. At the forest's edge, the samurai came to a house where a woman had blood on her arm and a man had a bandage on his neck. Without hesitation, the samurai killed them. He knew they were the evil shape-shifting wolves."

With Grandfather's words rattling through my head, I whisper, "Shape-shifter," and stand very still.

Yoshi laughs. "No way! What does Sensei say?"

Sensei had a pet wolf when he was a boy. "When I yelled at it, it whimpered," our teacher said. "When I yelled at it again, it bit me. Only a wild dog is wise enough to teach with its teeth. The wolf is a not a shape-shifter. The wolf is a mountain dog." Sensei's teeth are old and yellow, pointed like a wolf. Teaching teeth.

Closing my eyes, I think of Grandfather and Sensei, both sleeping in the sun. Which one do I believe? Ki-Yaga winks at me. He's right, of course.

Pitching my voice soft and low, I mimic Sensei. "The most dangerous creature is man."

Yoshi grins. "If you're the scariest thing in this forest with me, then I'm not afraid."

I wish I was brave like Yoshi.

"Something strange is happening. The animals know, and I can feel it. Maybe there is a danger here," I say. My imagination starts to run, and I walk faster to keep up with it.

Yoshi shrugs. He starts to sing loudly; he's not worried at all. His voice soars out over the valley.

Gray sky turns murky yellow-green, the way it sometimes does before a storm. The wind rises, and I feel my face change color to match the sky.

When I told Sensei how the thunder and lightning frightened me, he yelled in my ear. "Who is louder? Me or the storm?" His eyes flashed like lightning.

I didn't need to think. My eardrums told me the answer.

"You are louder, Master."

Sensei nodded. "Yes. And you are not afraid of me."

I felt better then, and I feel better now. If my voice

didn't scrape like fingernails on bamboo, I would sing with Yoshi. Whenever I sing, my friends tease me.

"Who trod on the cat's tail?" Taji sticks his fingers in his ears.

"Sometimes it's okay to squash a cockroach," says Mikko.

I am feeling braver, and I decide to ask Yoshi the unasked question.

"Yosh?"

Yoshi is singing so loud, he doesn't hear me.

"Yoshi!" I shout.

"You don't have to yell," he says.

I do, but a movement in the undergrowth silences me. *Tanuki.* Another shape-shifting dog of the darkness. It's small and fat like a badger, but secretive and shadowy like the wolf. Its unearthly wail pierces the gloom. *Tanuki* don't bark—they scream. My stomach knots, and my heart smashes into my chest. Shrieking, the *tanuki* runs across the path in front of me and down the cliff.

It's just a dog, I remind myself.

The wind howls, long and low. Like a wolf.

"I'm frightened," I whisper. The White Crane huddles in the grass.

"Walk closer. You're safe with me," Yoshi says, scanning the shadows for movement. He's worried now.

If I don't keep talking, the silence will swallow us both.

"Why won't you fight?" My voice is thin and squeaky. Scared.

Beneath our feet, the ground shakes and trembles. Earthquake!

Cra-ack! My crutch snaps. I try to catch myself and step back where the path's edge is crumbly and dry. My one foot slips into the air. The White Crane frantically flaps its wings.

"No-o-o!" Yoshi screams. "Not again!"

Down the mountain I roll. Like an egg.

Faster and faster. Over and over. Dust fills my nostrils and gathers in my ears. Around and around until everywhere hurts. The roaring earthquake fills my head with darkness.

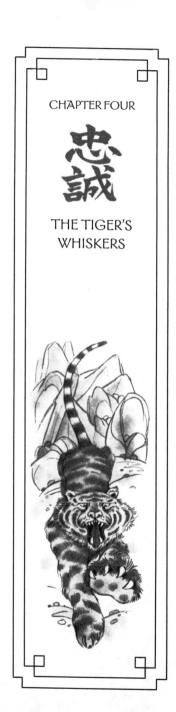

CHAPTER FOUR

忠誠

THE TIGER'S
WHISKERS

I can hear someone groaning. It's me.

A great shadow looms over my head. I cringe as the shape crouches, ready to spring. Instead it purrs inside my ear.

"Go to sleep, Niya."

Claws extended, it prods my blanket around me, before slinking back toward the cliff edge. Then, with a growl, it disappears down the mountain, leaving me to sleep in peace.

When I open my eyes again, I realize I'm back on the path, huddled beside Yoshi, my head thumping louder than Sensei's drum.

"Are you all right?" Yoshi asks.

I'm not, but I nod anyway. Now I know how a squashed cockroach feels.

"What happened? I thought I fell off the mountain."

"You did," replies Yoshi. "I climbed down and carried you back up. I almost fell off myself." Yoshi's face is striped with orange-brown mud.

I sneak a look over the cliff edge and see the slide of my fall. It's a long way. Looking makes my head spin. When I press my hands hard over my ears, the spinning slows and the thumping dulls.

"Thanks. You saved my life."

When we began the journey to the village, Yoshi and I were friends. Now we're samurai blood brothers, lashed together like bamboo poles in a raft. Where Yoshi leads, I'll follow.

"It was a long climb," he says. "Night fell before I was back. Then, when I tucked your blanket around you, I saw you didn't have your sword. So I went down again to search for it."

A samurai kid keeps his heart and soul in his sword. The thought of my blade abandoned on the mountain punches me in the stomach. My fingers reach for Izuru's hilt, and the White Crane's feathers flutter reassuringly against my hand.

"Double thanks. I owe you."

"You sure do." Yoshi grins. "While you were snoring, I made a list of things you can do to repay me — polish my chopsticks, lick my sandals clean, give me your desserts for a month . . ."

Making a rude noise, I let him know what I think of his list.

Yoshi grins wide, like the cat that swallowed the sparrow. "I have a secret," he says.

"What? Tell me."

"Guess."

I can't think of anything, so I throw my sandal at his nose.

"I'm not going to just tell you," he teases as he tosses it back even harder. "You're supposed to be smart. You have to figure it out."

I will. Even if it takes all the way down to the village. The early morning sun reminds me that a day has been lost under the earthquake. It's quieter inside my head now, so I struggle my way upright.

"Are you okay to walk?" Yoshi offers me his arm to lean on.

His other arm hangs crooked by his side.

"What happened to your arm?" I hadn't noticed before. Yoshi is good at hiding things he doesn't want other people to know. He's got more than one secret.

"Stupid accident. I climb down and up a cliff face twice and nothing happens. Then I trip over a small rock in the dark and this. . . ."

He grimaces as he shows me where it hurts. I know what to do. All samurai are experts when it comes to bones. You break lots of them if you train as often and hard as a samurai kid. Since I came to the Cockroach Ryu, I have broken a finger, my right arm, and my nose. My nose should be indestructible, the number of times I fall on it when I'm training. But once Taji swung his wooden practice sword and I wasn't paying attention—*smash.* Flatter than a rice pancake.

"My arm can wait until we get to the village," says Yoshi.

His strained white face tells me it can't. This isn't Yoshi's big secret. He's not smiling now.

"I need some twine and a splint." I can use bamboo.

It grows all over the mountain, and you can use it for everything. You can even eat it! Bamboo pickles are second only to honey pudding and vanilla rice cream.

With Yoshi holding me steady, I swing Izuru to cut two poles from a small bamboo clump uprooted by the earthquake. A short stem for Yoshi's arm and a larger one to replace my broken crutch. After chewing slices of bamboo to soften the fibers, we twist them into string.

Yoshi lies flat on the ground with his arm out straight. Carefully feeling along the bone, I find a lump but no break. I push harder to be sure.

"Sorry," I whisper as Yoshi grunts in pain. "I'll bind it to the splint so it doesn't hurt so much."

"Thanks," Yoshi mumbles through clenched teeth.

He's braver than me. The White Crane cringes in sympathy as it remembers its broken wing. When Sensei set my arm, I screamed like a *tanuki* dog.

Something important tugs at my memory. Yoshi bellowing as I fell off the mountain.

"Why did you yell 'Not again'?" I ask.

Watching Yoshi's face crease in pain, I wish I'd kept my mouth shut.

"It's because of me Sensei sent us racing an earthquake down the mountain," he says. "It was my fault you fell off the cliff."

I shrug. "It must've been something important. You don't have to talk about it if you don't want to."

This isn't Yoshi's secret, either. His shaking voice and sad eyes tell me this is an older, deeper secret.

Yoshi takes a deep breath. "I need to."

I wait quietly while he wrestles with the words. It's a harder fight than any competition event. Finally he speaks.

"I didn't grow up in a town, like you. Before the *ryu,* I lived in a mountain village, even smaller than the one below. One day, I was in a wrestling match with my friend. I was seven years old and he was ten, but I was much bigger than him. I threw him for the match point, and he hit his head on a rock."

Silence sits between us.

"He died." Yoshi coughs to hide the tears choking his throat. It's as quiet and eerie as the time before the earthquake. Something equally powerful is happening.

"The wrestling ring overlooked the rice fields. When

his dead body rolled over the edge, they wouldn't let me help bring it back. I was just a kid. I had to wait."

"It wasn't your fault. It was an accident."

Yoshi looks at me sadly.

"It doesn't help to know you accidentally killed someone. It feels as bad as if I did it on purpose."

"You went down the mountainside this time. You rescued me. It cancels out."

He doesn't look convinced, but he doesn't argue.

"I don't want to fight again," he mumbles, turning away to hide his wet eyes.

"You don't have to." I pat him on the back, hoping it will help.

"At the Trainee Games, our team will lose a point for every event I don't enter."

He's right, and we need every point we can get. Last year we were novices, but this time, we'll have passed through our Coming-of-Age Ceremony. We will be warrior-level trainees. The rules will be different. When someone wins an event, they'll get a point. If someone doesn't complete an event, the team will be penalized a point. We'll be lucky to score a zero.

Yoshi looks miserable. "I'll be letting everyone down. Even Taji is competing in archery, and he can't see the target."

"It doesn't matter if you don't wrestle or sword fight. Sensei says there's more to being a samurai than combat skills. What about origami, haiku poetry, or calligraphy? You're good at all those. Maybe you will win a point."

He still looks sad.

"It doesn't matter, Yosh. Being together in a team is the important thing. We're not going to slay any Dragons. Unless they laugh themselves senseless watching us try. When they see me hopping around the ring . . . Hey! It might work. I think our chances are improving."

Yoshi tries to grin, but his smile slips off and lands at my foot.

When I am sad, I like to walk. Levering myself up with the bamboo pole, I hope walking will help Yoshi, too.

"Let's go. We need to collect the supplies and get back to the *ryu*. Sensei might need us," I say.

We know Sensei and our friends are safe. Cockroaches are very hard to kill, our master told us. It would take more than a mountain shifting to exterminate them.

The path is broken and twisted, crumpled like the pieces of paper Kyoko tosses aside when she is trying to make an origami cockroach. Leaning against each other for support, Yoshi and I climb over mashed mounds of dirt and stones. The big flat halfway rock is gone, and a pile of rubble sits in its place. Newly chipped edges push and poke at the bottom of our straw sandals, but they're no match for Kyoko's clever weaving. Kyoko makes all our sandals, and an extra finger means an extra strand of straw. Our sandals are tough as leather.

It's getting harder to find the path.

"It is never easy to know which path to take," Sensei says. "But once the path is taken, it will tell your feet where to go. And if you do not have two feet, it will tell your one foot twice."

My foot is a good listener, so I lead the way down.

Lizards rustle in the undergrowth. Birds startle as we detour through the grass and inside a hollow tree stump I see two snakes. It's a lucky sign to see two together. The mountain is at peace again. No *tanuki*. No wolf. No dogs at all.

Some people have a dog for their spirit totem. I'm glad my totem is the White Crane; dogs have too many teeth. Then I realize what Yoshi's secret is. There's only one thing that would give him the courage to tell me why he doesn't fight.

"Yoshi! You've found your spirit totem. What is it?"

He grins and growls softly, like a great cat.

"It's the Tiger," I whoop. I would dance too if I could. The Tiger is a powerful spirit. "You are strong and clever. And your face is beginning to grow hair in scruffy tufts — like the Tiger's whiskers."

He takes a swipe at me with his good arm, but his smile tells me I'm right.

"Missed me," I tease, ducking out of his way.

Time passes quickly when you have a friend to lean on. When we reach the lower slopes, the path is undisturbed and I'm walking as if I never fell off the mountain.

The tremors haven't touched the rice field terraces. Here the crop is green and healthy. The rich valley soil keeps the people well fed, with a ready surplus for sale and trade. That'll be good news for our stomachs when the winter snow falls.

The village in front of us is a large settlement of more than twenty-five houses. The thing I like best about the village is the noise. Except when Sensei's banging his drum, it's very quiet at the *ryu*. Sensei doesn't like to be disturbed when he's sleeping.

"How can I get any work done if you keep waking me up?" he asks.

Yoshi and I thread our way through stray chickens, yapping dogs, and people coming and going in every direction. An enormous ox stands in the middle of the street. Keeping an eye on its powerful back legs, we edge our way around.

"Hey!" I call to a boy about our age, standing with the ox. "Which way is the market today?"

The market is never in the same place.

"That way." He gestures down the road. "It's a long hop for a samurai kid."

"You should be careful you don't stand too close to that ox's back legs. Otherwise you might be hopping, too," retorts Yoshi.

The village boy points at me and laughs. "Is that how you lost your leg?"

I take a deep breath and pull my hat down over my face so no one can see.

"*Om*-grrrh," I swear into the bamboo.

Yoshi places his arm on mine. "Ignore him. Have you still got the list in your head?"

I nod. It takes more than an egg roll down a cliff face to make me forget things.

First we visit the Village Chief and exchange two bottles of *dokudami* wine for a letter of credit.

"Greetings, young samurai." The Chief bows low.

We bow lower to show our respect.

"I wish your master health and good fortune." He bows even lower for Sensei. The Chief's nose touches the ground. It's a good thing there is no one more respected than Sensei or we would all be lying face-first in the dirt. The Chief gives me a piece of rice paper with a number on it. It tells the market sellers how

"Greetings, young samurai."

much we have to spend. Other buyers use coins but not us. Samurai aren't allowed to handle money.

"A samurai serves because it is his duty. Not because he desires gold coins," Sensei told us.

"How will he eat, then?" Mikko asked.

"With his mouth," Sensei answered.

Our teacher is skinny like a chopstick, but he eats a lot. He can slurp down honey rice pudding faster than me. Once I saw him mop the bowl with his beard and suck the pudding from it until it was clean and white again.

We work our way through the bustle to the far end where the women lay out goods on rows of bamboo mats under the trees.

"It's Ki-Yaga's kids. Have some cherry blossom gum." Chattering like birds, they help us select our purchases.

"How is your good master?" they ask as they pack the items into Yoshi's harness.

By now our mouths are stuffed full of sweets and we can only mumble.

"Ki-Yaga must be very old," a gray-haired woman says. "He was old when I was young."

"I thought he was dead," exclaims another. "Didn't he die last winter?"

The first one puts her finger to her lips. "Hush, don't say such things."

"You can't kill that one," interrupts an ancient crone. "He's not human."

"Shhh, Grandmother," Gray-Hair clucks. "Don't mind her," she whispers to us. "She's very feeble."

The crone won't be shushed. She goes on.

"Your master sends a message. He says the Little Cockroaches are safe, and he is pleased to see a smile on the face of his Tiger."

"How do you know that?" I demand.

"A little bird told me. Birds sing to other birds. This old raven squawks in the White Crane's ear," she answers, winking.

"What bird told you? Sensei is not a bird."

The old woman cackles so hard she spits bits of bean curd on her sandals. "He's a *tengu* crow, that's what he is. An old black demon bird with wrinkled goblin feet.

56

A fallen samurai priest from the dark side. Have a look at your master's feet." Coughing and spluttering, she doubles over with screeching laughter.

Sensei's feet *are* elderly and wrinkled like claws, but it's because he's very old, not because he's a *tengu* goblin from the mountain.

The commotion attracts the Chief's attention.

"Please ignore our old one. Her brain is egg yolk. She means no disrespect," he says.

He gives his nose a scrape in the dirt to apologize. Still bowing, he leads the old woman away from the mats.

"What do you think about that?" I whisper to Yoshi.

"Old fishwife tales."

I remember what Sensei said about *dokudami*. Magic smells fishy to the noses of men. But Sensei's nose can't smell *dokudami*. Maybe it isn't about thick nostril hair. Maybe he's not a man at all.

"Sensei can see with his eyes closed," I say.

"That's because he's a wizard. They learn things like that. You know what I think?" The Tiger grins, ready to pounce.

"What?"

"I think you must have hit your head recently. You're thinking crooked."

Yoshi's right. Sometimes I let my imagination run away, like I did yesterday on the mountain.

"Let's go look at swords," I say, linking arms with my friend.

CHAPTER FIVE

義

THE SWORD
MASTER

"We're not the only customers this morning." Yoshi points to a sword hanging outside Master Onaku's door.

Golden dragons stalk the blade's scabbard, breathing fire studded with precious stones. Silver rivers run beneath their feet. Someone rich and powerful is inside the smithy.

When a samurai goes into a building, he leaves his sword outside. If anyone touches a samurai sword, even accidentally, the penalty is instant death. Sensei told us the tale of a warrior who went visiting and forgot to remove his sword.

"This is a very sad story," he said. "One day a samurai went to dine at his friend's home, where the lady of the house was famous for her honey rice pudding. As the friend sat down to dinner, he bumped the samurai's

60

sword and . . ." We all ducked as Sensei swung an imaginary blade in front of our noses. "*Swish. Swish.* The friend fell dead on the floor. The samurai was never invited back."

Sensei sighed into his beard. "It was a terrible tragedy. Never to taste such pudding again. Listen carefully, Little Cockroaches. He who remembers what Bushido teaches will never miss out on great desserts."

Yoshi and I remember the story and lean our swords against the wall.

"I don't need this anymore." Yoshi unfastens his bamboo splint and stands it beside the swords. He stretches his arm and flicks his wrist. "It feels better now."

"That was quick. Probably nothing wrong with your arm in the first place. You just wanted my sympathy," I joke.

But Yoshi is serious.

"You bound it well. I'm glad you were there to help me."

Standing inside the smithy is a tall, dark man in a red silk traveling cloak embroidered with gold thread. He has removed his battle helmet, revealing long black hair bound up in a warrior topknot. A narrow scar runs down the side of his weasel-thin face.

He turns to nod, but when he sees it is us, he looks over our heads and then away. Little Cockroaches are beneath the gaze of the Master of the Dragon Ryu.

Oblivious to his visitors, the swordsmith is crafting a new blade. As he works, he chants the story of a legendary sword locked into stone. I want to listen, but Onaku's singing is even worse than mine. Covering my ears would be impolite, so I grit my teeth and hum inside my head. *Om. Om. Om.*

"An honorable sword sings loudly with truth and purity," Sensei teaches.

No wonder Master Onaku's swords are so prized. They are born singing at the top of their lungs to drown out their maker's awful voice.

An arsenal of weapons hangs on the walls. My fingers itch to touch the dual weapons of samurai combat: the long, curved *katana* and the short, pointed *wakizashi*. A sword and dagger. After my Coming-of-Age Ceremony, both will hang from my belt. Three days is such a long time to wait.

It's warm in the smithy, where a large charcoal fire burns in one corner. I take off my traveling coat, fold it into a cushion, and sit down on a mat to wait. Yoshi does the same. A padded seat is much more comfortable than a bony backside. Some swords take a long time to forge, and it's a great insult to interrupt a master craftsman at work.

The Dragon Master has no respect for the sword making.

"You, swordsmith!" he yells.

Master Onaku continues working.

"I will not be ignored!" The Dragon Master's angry voice roars through the workshop. He thumps his fist against the wall in rage. Two swords, a small dagger, and a large package fall to the dirt floor.

Master Onaku raises his head to glare but doesn't stop.

"Bring me the goods I have ordered!" the Dragon Master shouts. "Get them NOW or I will swing my sword to cut off your head!"

Beside me, the Tiger tenses ready to spring. Touching Yoshi gently, I let him know I'll defend Onaku's honor with him.

Master Onaku puts down his half-finished sword and points to the package the Dragon knocked off the wall.

"You're not the only sword maker on this island," the Dragon hisses as he bends to pick up his swords. When he stands upright, he is directly in front of Onaku, almost touching. Suddenly, despite the fire, there's a coldness in the air.

"They say Master Yuri makes a sword that can split the hair on a man's head." The Dragon's words spit and splatter in the Sword Master's face.

Onaku shrugs and wipes the spittle from his cheeks. "If you wish to take up hair cutting, it's none of my business. My swords are for splitting a man's head, not trimming his hair."

The temperature in the smithy rises. The Dragon is as furious as fire. With a loud clunk, a bag of coins lands at Onaku's feet.

"Count it if you like," the Dragon Master sneers.

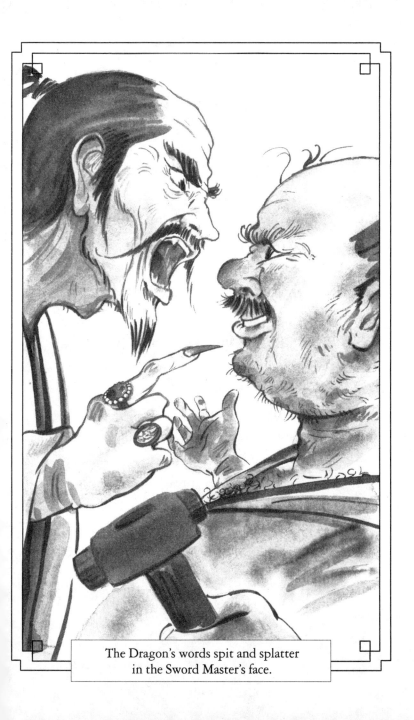

The Dragon's words spit and splatter
in the Sword Master's face.

Onaku stands still. Like a sword poised above its victim.

The point of the sword is very sharp. Sensei's words ring inside my head.

Slinging the package over his shoulder, the Dragon Master steps back. His face twisting in anger, he knows he can't win this battle.

"May your blades bend and snap in two," he says. "The Dragon Ryu will purchase its swords elsewhere in the future."

The words slice through the air, but Onaku is as steely as his swords.

"May your flames fizzle and fart," he responds.

I clamp my hand over my mouth to catch my laughter before it escapes.

"Out of my way, roaches." The Dragon pushes past us.

At the doorway, he turns. Dark reptilian eyes glitter, and his tongue flicks over his lips.

I hold my breath.

"I will see you two at the Samurai Trainee Games," he snarls through white, pointed teeth. "Perhaps I will find you squashed on the sole of my sandal."

"Grrrr." Beside me, the Tiger growls. The White Crane snaps its beak, and I'm ready to peck out the Dragon's eyes.

With a rustle of red silk and a threatening wave of his sword, the Dragon Master is gone.

Swish. Chop. Yoshi draws a line across his neck using his finger as a blade. "Those Dragons won't know what hit them when they meet us at the Games," he says.

I imagine the Dragon Master's helmet rolling on the floor and give it a good kick with my one, strong leg.

Master Onaku's ruined sword skids across the dirt and lands in the trash heap. Now the Sword Master is ready to talk.

"Welcome, Niya. Welcome, Yoshi. I apologize for the rudeness of my customer." He bows low.

We bow lower, smudging our foreheads with dirt.

"You are brave. The Dragon Master is a powerful man," I say. Yoshi nods.

The Sword Master laughs — a warm, honey-filled sound that drips down the back of our throats.

Master Onaku is a familiar face. Twice a year he comes to the *ryu* to visit Sensei. To cleanse his soul and get away from his wife, he says. Onaku is short and broad like a tree stump. He has a round, red face, a big nose, and the most beautiful wife in the world. Sensei says he built his *ryu* in the Tateyama Mountains so he could be close to Onaku's swords. Onaku Cays he built his smithy in the village so he could be close to the *ryu*'s wine.

"I am not afraid of him," the Sword Master says. "He huffs and blows nothing but smoke rings that stink in the air. No sword will sing for the Dragon Master. There's no skill in bullying others. Now, if your master yelled at me, I would hide under the table. Ki-Yaga would not allow his trainees to fight with swords that mutter and mumble."

I look at Yoshi. We have an advantage over the Dragons! Their swords are weak, and ours are strong.

"Now, boys," Onaku says, "I must begin a new sword. Would you like to stay for lunch and watch me work?"

"Yes, Master," we chorus. "It is a great honor to be invited." Our stomachs want to stay, too.

Yoshi and I sit back down. Behind us, a screen door

slides open and Mrs. Onaku places trays of food on our mat—sticky rice wrapped in bamboo leaves and sugar soy cake.

Mrs. Onaku smells like cherry blossoms, and when she smiles, goldfish turn somersaults in my stomach. At the spring cherry blossom celebrations, the old men begin with a saying, "The food is better than the flower." When I look at Mrs. Onaku, I know they've got it wrong. She's a great cook and a beautiful flower. One is not better than the other at all.

"I thought I heard the sound of Ki-Yaga's boys. I hope you're hungry," she says.

"Yes, Mrs. Onaku. Thank you." The food smell tickles and teases my nostrils. I try not to drool.

"Tell your master he needs to send his students to visit more often." She smiles, and the goldfish in my stomach do backflips.

My face pink like the blossom, I bow low to hide my embarrassment. When Mrs. Onaku is gone, I lift my face off the mat.

"There's straw in your hair and egg on your chin." Yoshi grins as he stuffs his mouth with cake.

I'd like to give him a shove, but I don't want to disturb the swordsmith.

"I'll get you later," I whisper.

Cake melts on my tongue and trickles, warm and sweet, down to the goldfish.

"She's a good cook." Rubbing his round belly, Master Onaku nods approvingly at our mouths crammed with food. "You know how I can tell I'm a smart man?" he asks.

We shake our heads. Our mouths are too full to make words.

"I married her. Smartest thing I ever did. Have you seen the Dragon Master's wife?"

We haven't, but Onaku's laughter tells us all we need to know.

The swordsmith sings while he works. Luckily, Onaku's barking voice is soon lost under the sound of his hammer smashing against steel. A samurai sword is made of two different layers of metal, folded and pummeled over and over again. Magic fills the smithy as Onaku's big hands twist and turn the metal and the battering rises to an almost unbearable crescendo. Sometimes magic is very loud.

When the hammering is finished, Onaku covers the raw blade with wet clay. Using long tongs, he holds it over the fire to bake. Then he lays the sword on a narrow bench. His strong arms swing a heavy mallet high above the blade. It's time for the clay to be broken open, to reveal the sword within. The Dragon Master's words hang in the air. I forget to breathe. Will the sword bend and break?

Crash.

A cloud of clay dust puffs skyward. Steam hisses as Onaku plunges the new blade into warm water. The Sword Master holds the finished sword aloft for us to see.

It sings to our samurai hearts. The Tiger purrs, and the White Crane stretches its wings. Secretly I hope the new sword is mine, but a samurai never sees his sword before it is presented at his Coming-of-Age Ceremony. Maybe this one is for Taji, or Mikko. Or Kyoko.

"It's beautiful," Yoshi says. I can only nod. It's more wonderful than words.

"Thank you." Onaku bows. "You need to leave now, so you reach the *ryu* before dark."

Yoshi unties the last bottle of wine from the harness and hands it to Onaku. "Our master sends you a gift."

Grinning, the swordsmith opens the flask and takes a big sniff.

I can't help asking. "Doesn't that smell awful?"

"Yes. It smells like being smacked in the nose with a rotten fish." He smiles and pats his ample belly. "But in my stomach it fizzes and tickles. Now boys, I will see you at the Ceremony."

"We look forward to your visit." I bow.

"Do you have a message for our master?" Yoshi asks, bowing too.

"No message," Onaku says.

We take our leave and begin the long walk home, racing the sun up the mountain. We'll be home by sunset.

When we reach the *ryu,* Sensei, Kyoko, Taji, and Mikko are waiting for us. Kyoko has something cupped in her hands.

Arms outstretched toward Yoshi, six fingers unfold like lotus blossom petals. The Dragon kids are wrong when they make fun of her. White hair and pink eyes aren't strange at all. Kyoko is a lotus flower girl.

In her palm sits a paper tiger.

"Thanks," says Yoshi, beaming. "How did you know I needed one of those?"

Kyoko grins and points at Sensei, who grins even wider.

Our family is complete. The Tiger, the Snow Monkey, the Golden Bat, the Striped Gecko, and me. I am the White Crane, and I wrap my wings around them all. Working together, our spirit totems are strong. Maybe even powerful enough to defeat a Dragon.

"Did you bring me a message from Onaku?" asks Sensei.

"No," I answer.

Sensei doesn't move. He's waiting. Yoshi raises his eyebrow at me, and I shrug.

"It's true. The Sword Master said, 'No message,'" Yoshi says.

"Aaaah. Now the message has been delivered.

Nothing is an answer. Have you already forgotten what I taught you, Niya?" asks Sensei.

I grin because I can see the trick. I am still the expert at this Zen stuff.

"I remember NOTHING," I declare.

Sensei is pleased.

"Good. Come, Little Cockroaches. Let us make tea." He strides off, laughing.

Groan. Double moan. Triple groan. There's nothing funny about the tea ceremony. Who wants to sit quietly and sip green tea when they've just returned from an exciting adventure? I want to laugh and chatter and tell everything we saw and did. I want to show off. Just a bit.

Kyoko giggles.

"What's so funny?" I ask.

She points. The teahouse is nothing but a pile of rubble. "The earthquake didn't like the tea ceremony, either."

Yoshi whistles. "Was anything else damaged?"

"Nothing except Sensei's favorite cherry tree. Its leaves are planted in the ground, and the roots are waving in the air. But he's not worried. Look." Mikko gestures with his one arm. Sensei is already curled up under an old, stooped plum tree, waiting for us to join him.

"Even without tea, we can still have cake," Sensei calls. "Where are those cakes you brought?"

Yoshi and I haven't mentioned the cakes Mrs. Onaku gave us. I give Yoshi a sideways glance.

"How did he know that?" I whisper.

"Mrs. Onaku always sends something," says Yoshi.

"Why are you whispering?" Kyoko asks.

"Some old woman in the village said Sensei was a *tengu* mountain goblin, and Niya thinks she might be right."

My friends laugh at me. *Caw, caw.* Running in a circle around me, Taji flaps his arms like wings.

"You think Sensei changes into a black crow when we're not looking?" Mikko splutters through laughter. "I thought you were the smart one."

"Well, he knows everything. Even when he's asleep," I protest.

Kyoko's eyes dance with mischief. "We could give him a test to see if he can fly."

"I don't think pushing him off a cliff would work. Niya is the White Crane, and he couldn't fly when he fell off the mountain," says Yoshi.

"Niya fell off the mountain?" Taji looks concerned. His eyes might not see but they can still talk. They tell me he cares.

"It's a long story," I say. "It's also the tale of how the Tiger caught Yoshi."

My friends crowd around, eager to listen.

"If I thought my master was a *tengu* bird goblin, I would not make him wait for his cake," Sensei shouts.

The White Crane believes in black crows. I decide not to take any risks. Storytelling and showing off can wait, but Sensei can't. My fingers fumble with the harness ties.

"Let me do that." Kyoko unravels the double-tied string as if it were a loose ribbon. An extra finger is great for undoing knots.

"Chop, chop," Sensei calls. "How can I get enough sleep when my stomach rumbles louder than an earth-quake?"

CHAPTER SIX

THE HORSE'S
MOUTH

A smell drifts across from the kitchen. It jumps in the window and thumps me on the nose. I sit bolt upright in bed, and sniff. It's pudding. Honey pudding. Not a whiff of rice pancakes. It's pudding and . . . and chicken noodles. Have I have slept until dinner?

Looking around the room, I see my friends, still asleep. The paper walls vibrate gently in time with Mikko's snoring. Behind the screen at the end of the room, Kyoko's slumbering shadow rolls over. It looks and sounds like an ordinary morning but it smells different.

"Mikko, wake up." I poke him in the belly. Grunting, he turns onto his stomach. "Yoshi, Kyoko, Taji. Wake up. Something strange is happening!" I shout.

One by one they open their eyes to stagger out of bed and sniff. Taji has the best nose. Without eyes, he uses his nose and his ears twice as hard as the rest of us. "It's definitely dinner," he announces.

Together we roll Mikko out of bed and onto the floor. His nose twitches. "What's that smell? Where's breakfast?"

"That's what we're trying to tell you!" Kyoko yells in his ear. Mikko's wide awake now.

It's not easy for a samurai kid to get dressed in a hurry. Lots of layers go over the cotton loincloth I sleep in. First, a kimono with a long sash to tie the folds together. Then a short jacket, with another sash. Finally, I drag on big, baggy trousers. Samurai are fashionable warriors. It's not enough to die honorably. You have to look good, too.

"Let's go." My crutch flying, I race toward the kitchen. The others soon pass me. Taji veers in front of Kyoko in the lead, and we all fall in a heap, arms and legs flailing.

"Watch out where you're running next time, Bat Boy." Kyoko pins Taji in a playful headlock.

"How am I supposed to see where I'm going?" Taji is our best wrestler. He can hear a move before it's made and easily flips Kyoko over, to hold her shoulders against the ground.

"I give in," she pants. "But you're still a lousy runner."

"Oww. Who's shoving their foot in my ear?" I yell. It's not Taji or Kyoko, and it's not big enough for Yoshi. It must be Mikko. I give his ankle a yank, and he moves his foot into my mouth. Remembering what Sensei said about teaching teeth, I take a small bite. Now Mikko will watch where he puts his feet!

"Yow-ow. Oww!" It's Mikko's turn to yell.

"Early morning wrestling practice. Excellent." Sensei nods approvingly from the kitchen doorway. "Double dessert for everyone."

Sensei has dinner bowls set out on the table — noodle bowls, little soy sauce dipping bowls, and, most important, bowls for pudding.

"Hurry, hurry," he says. "We have much practicing to do. In three days you leave to journey to the Games. Eat quickly, for soon it will be lunch and then it will be breakfast. Today we eat backward."

"Why are we doing that?" I ask.

"So when we get to breakfast, there will still be plenty of time left to practice. Chop, chop, Little Cockroaches."

"A master walks a fine line between wisdom and

insanity," Sensei once told me. I think he just fell headfirst over the line.

"A samurai must discipline himself so his body does not question what his mind decides," Sensei continues.

I always think with my stomach. It never listens to my head, and nothing will change that.

Yoshi isn't convinced, either. "What if it gets dark? We can't practice in the dark."

"Why not?" Taji grins. "Makes no difference to me. I'm always in the dark."

If Taji can do it, then so can I. My head tells my gut to stop rumbling and rudely interrupting.

Sensei picks up a glass and drinks half the plum juice.

"Is the glass half empty or half full?" He holds it up for us to see.

My stomach knows this one. Before I was dying of hunger; now I'm dying of thirst.

"The glass is half full," I say, wishing I was drinking the rest now.

"You could say the glass is half empty," Kyoko muses. "If you wanted more."

I do want more. She's right, the glass is half empty. Suddenly it makes sense: I can choose.

"So is it dinner or breakfast?" Sensei asks. "Will the mind tell the body pudding or pancakes?"

It's an easy choice. "Dinner," we chorus.

We shovel down our food. Halfway through my second pudding, Sensei bangs on his drum. Dinner is over.

"Stop eating now. More practice!" Sensei waves us toward the door.

No way! I'm not leaving my dessert. I empty my soy sauce into a nearby bonsai plant, then wipe the bowl clean with the corner of my kimono. Then I tip the pudding into the bowl and gently place it in my pocket. I'll finish my dessert outside.

But there's no time to eat.

"This way." With long spidery steps, Sensei strides toward the field behind the kitchen. Even Yoshi has to hurry to keep up.

Uma, the horse, grazes in the long grass. For once, I wish I was back in the classroom writing calligraphy. Some kids think horseback riding is fun. Not us. Not with Sensei's crazy horse.

Uma is cranky and cantankerous. He's really old, but he throws tantrums like a two-year-old. Nostrils twitching, he's staring at me now. I'm sure Uma knows what I'm thinking. Flicking his mane, he snorts in my direction, and a fine spray of nostril mist settles on my hand. *Yeech!* Horse snot. I wipe it on the grass.

Sensei smiles. "He likes you."

He doesn't. Uma turns away and swipes his tail across his backside. It's a big insult, to be no more important than a fly on his rump.

Sensei's horse hates being ridden. When Kyoko puts the saddle on him, he throws it off. When Mikko loops the reins over his neck, he tosses them away. And when we try to climb on, he throws us, too.

Many years ago, before I was born, a wounded samurai came to the Cockroach Ryu. Sensei cared for him, and when he left, he gave Sensei his only valuable possession. This crazy horse.

"In his glory days, Uma was a warrior steed." Sensei strokes the horse's thick mane. "He raced into battle and trampled on fallen swords. He doesn't like teaching trainees to ride. Your bony knees make him grumpy."

Sensei takes an apple from behind his beard and feeds it to Uma. If I did that, Uma would be crunching my fingers. He curls his lip in a toothy smile. Big yellow teaching teeth stare at me. Sensei looks, too. Together, the horse and its wizard read my mind.

"You can learn a lot from teeth," Sensei says. "Especially when they bite."

"That's true." Grinning at Mikko, I remember this morning's wrestle.

"What does it mean, if he bites?" Kyoko asks.

Mikko knows. "It means stop."

Sensei nods. "If you can ride a horse that does not want you, you can ride anything. Even a Dragon. First you have to find a weakness. What is Mikko's weakness?"

I know because I practice with Mikko every day.

"Shoulder weight thrust off the back right foot." It gets him all the time. Luckily for me, the right foot is the one I've still got.

"Is that how you beat me?" Mikko is really smart when he bothers to think. His lazy brain is ticking fast. Tomorrow I'll have to find something new if I want to beat him again.

Sensei twists his beard around his finger. "Very good, Niya. But what would a Dragon think?"

"That Mikko's one arm is his weakness," answers Taji.

"Yes. Foolish Dragon, even blinder than my Golden Bat."

Taji beams. He's proud of his spirit totem. Rare and clever, the Golden Bat doesn't need to see where it's going. It knows.

"A weakness is not always obvious. Find Uma's weakness and you will ride," instructs Sensei. "Until then . . . more practice!"

Waving his staff in Uma's direction, our teacher wanders off to sit under the large, shady maple tree, where he can watch us from his sleep.

Catching Uma is never easy. Facing away from us, he doesn't need to see what we are doing. He knows. Uma is like the Golden Bat.

"Let's get this over and done with," I sigh.

"You go first," Kyoko suggests. "He likes you best."

Probably because I only have one knee. It makes him half as grumpy.

Uma has his head down in the grass, pretending not to listen.

"Easy, boy," I say, holding out my hand. He lets me strap on the saddle and climb onto his back. Kyyaa! Raising my arm triumphantly, I am a legendary samurai rider.

But Uma is not in the mood for even one knee, no matter how legendary. I land with a thump. A cold splash soaks through my layers of clothing — through the jacket, the baggy pants, and the kimono. My fingers sink into a wet sticky mess. Oh, no! I forgot about my pudding.

Uma's nose twitches as he bends to sniff my hand. Scooping the remainder out of my pocket, I offer it to him. His tongue is rough and tickles my palm while he slurps down my leftover dessert. A warm, sticky muzzle rubs against my neck. Uma's weakness is the same as mine — honey pudding!

"He likes honey pudding!" I call, leading my new friend back to the others.

Kyoko doesn't look convinced.

"Go on. You try." I scrape the remaining sticky mess from my pocket and smear it on her hand.

Uma licks his lips as Kyoko climbs into the saddle. She reaches around to offer her hand. He slurps happily.

"Let's go, boy." Kyoko nudges gently with her knee.

Uma is on our side now and is happy to let Kyoko ride him to the cherry tree and back. As long as we've got enough pudding.

"At least now we won't fall off our horse at the Games. One less thing for the other teams to laugh at," says Mikko.

I try not to think about the Games, but it must be hardest for Mikko. Once he was a mighty Dragon, a winner. Now he is one of us.

"Do you miss the Dragon Ryu?" I ask him.

"Never." Mikko shakes his head.

"It must have felt good to win sometimes." Kyoko sounds wistful.

Mikko shakes his head even harder. "When a Dragon makes a mistake, the Master strikes him hard across the head with his fist. When a Cockroach gets it wrong, Sensei cares. He says, 'More practice!'"

"More practice!" Sensei yells from his sleep.

Suddenly it feels good to be a loser Cockroach. It feels safe.

Uma bares his teeth. A big toothy grin speckled with pudding. Drab and cockroach brown like our kimonos, he's one of us, too. Sensei says brown is good. A samurai must earn attention from his skill with weapons and words, not the bright colors he wears.

"Students who want people to notice what they are wearing should wear nothing. Everyone looks then," Sensei told us.

Still, I wish I had a magnificent red and gold silk cloak like the Dragon Master. Sensei has a long dark brown cotton cloak, stained with cherry juice and torn at the corner Taji accidentally stood on. I don't want one like that.

After horseback riding, it's lunch. Even eating backward, lunch is still in the middle. We rush through it and stuff our faces with plums.

The afternoon lesson is archery. I'm good at it,

because I am the White Crane, expert at standing still. Even on one leg. Archery is about balance.

A samurai bow is taller than a man and my bow is a head taller than me. Sensei helps us carve our bows from the *ryu* trees. We make bamboo arrows and tie a feather to the end. When I nock my arrow and send it flying skyward in an arc, the White Crane opens its wings and flies with it.

In the old days, when Ki-Yaga was a hero, samurai archers rode horses. I want to be a hero this afternoon, but Uma is nowhere to be seen. A handful of pudding loyalty doesn't last all day.

Our practice area is a large clearing in the middle of the forest, behind the classroom where Sensei is meditating. The hardest thing about archery is ignoring the rustling noises. It's especially hard for me because I have a vivid imagination.

There really is a monster out there. Black Tusk, the most fearsome wild pig in Japan, lives in our forest. None of us have ever seen him, but Sensei has.

"What should we do if we see the boar?" Yoshi asked.

"Run. Run fast to the tallest cherry tree," Sensei said.

Behind me, the undergrowth crackles and rustles.

"Face this way." Mikko points Taji in the direction of the target. Taji places an arrow in the bow, pulls the string back, and lets the bamboo fly. *Twang. Phlock!* It pierces the outermost edge, but Taji can't see it almost missed, and we always say the same thing.

"Well done," Yoshi calls. Kyoko claps.

The snuffling sounds are loud and close. His bow and arrows forgotten, Taji is listening hard.

Black Tusk charges from the undergrowth.

"Eeeeee!" Kyoko's high-pitched shriek claws at my eardrum.

"Run!" yells Yoshi, dragging me along with him. I can't run fast enough. The boar's hot breath burns the back of my leg. My wooden crutch is not made for racing wild pigs. I imagine my skin beginning to rip. I imagine a warm trickle of blood.

Yoshi sweeps me onto his back, like an empty harness package. The boar runs faster. Wild animals can smell the weakest member of a pack. The boar smells me. Clinging to Yoshi's back, the White Crane shivers in fear.

Kyoko reaches the cherry tree first, with Taji close behind. They help pull Mikko out of danger. It's easy to run with one arm, but it's hard to climb. Yoshi pushes me upward, and my friends haul me onto a large branch. Yoshi scrambles up after me. Five samurai kids safely perched in a tree.

"Thanks," I say when I can breathe again. "You're a hero, Yosh."

"Now what?" says Mikko.

Yoshi shrugs. "We wait."

"Shoo, shoo!" Kyoko yells and waves her fists.

Black Tusk claws at the tree. Staring into its big, hairy face, I see eyes filled with hate. What it hates is us.

"We're stuck here," moans Kyoko.

"At least we won't be missing dinner. We've already had that," Mikko jokes.

"Sensei said we choose how we look at things. Maybe we should enjoy the view," suggests Taji.

That's a pretty smart idea, considering Taji can't see. Sensei would be pleased.

From the top of the cherry tree, I can see for miles. The *ryu* buildings are old and dilapidated — the

Yoshi pushes me upward, and my friends
haul me onto a large branch.

kitchen, Sensei's room beside the teahouse rubble, our sleeping quarters and classroom. In the center of the buildings, the practice ring is surrounded by even older trees.

"There are a lot of cherry and plum trees," Yoshi comments.

Kyoko hugs her branch. "I'm glad this one's here."

"Maybe Sensei put it here for harmony," says Taji. "To provide balance with the buildings."

When you put things in certain places to create harmony, good things happen. Water brings peace and purity, so my mother puts fishbowls everywhere, even in doorways. It's not easy to hop around fishbowls on the floor, but it's even harder to jump flopping goldfish.

"Let's ask Sensei, after he rescues us." Mikko points to the edge of field.

Sensei sits astride Uma. A skinny old man on a crazy old horse. The boar looks up but sees nothing to be afraid of. Silly pig.

"Zaa! Zaa!" Sensei screeches, charging toward us, his beard flapping wildly. The terrified boar doesn't look again. It rushes, squealing, into the forest. Everything runs when Sensei yells. Not just us.

"I see you have been practicing sprinting. Excellent," Sensei says. "Breakfast is ready. Rice pancakes and syrup." He digs his pointy crow feet into Uma's flank, and they gallop toward the *ryu*.

We climb down and follow, racing through the sunset toward the kitchen. As if a wild boar is chasing us.

CHAPTER SEVEN

THE BOY FROM THE VILLAGE

"People are coming! People are coming!" Yoshi shouts from his meditation stone. Yoshi's stone juts way out over the valley. He likes to sit right out on the end and watch the sunrise.

It makes me dizzy to look at him, but he says it helps him think. I know he thinks about that day on the path when he saved my life and that other day long ago when his friend died. He's balancing more than his body out on the edge of the rock.

"Who is it?" Kyoko is faster than the rest of us and reaches the stone first. Even with my crutch, I'm last, of course.

Four of us strain to see into the valley. We don't get many visitors. Sometimes old friends come to visit Sensei, like Master Onaku, the swordsmith. And once my mother and father came to check on me.

"He is a good boy. He listens well and eats everything on his plate," Sensei said. My teacher knows exactly what to say to parents. Mother and Father were proud. I could imagine them repeating Sensei's words in tearooms across Japan, to their friends and anyone who would listen. Little Niya, praised so highly by the great Ki-Yaga.

I peer down the valley path. "There are a lot of them, at least ten." With excellent eyesight, the White Crane can spot a beetle from the air.

Yoshi leans so far over the edge, he makes us all nervous. "They're carrying something. Someone on a stretcher," he reports.

"I'll go and get Sensei." Taji sprints back toward the classroom, where our master is preparing the afternoon lessons.

By the time Taji returns with Sensei, the band of villagers has almost reached the *ryu*.

"Mikko, Niya. Go and greet our visitors. Yoshi, help with the stretcher. Kyoko, come with me to ready the healing table." Sensei's arms wave wildly, like a squid kite in the wind.

Yoshi rushes ahead to meet the stretcher, with Mikko and I hurrying behind him. The front bearer is a small woman, her expression blank with worry and exhaustion. She nods gratefully when Yoshi takes her corner.

"What can we do to help you?" I ask.

"My son needs Master Ki-Yaga's aid." She points to the young boy lying on the stretcher, his face white with pain. "Not much longer, Riaze," his mother comforts him. "The Master will make it right."

Riaze's face is familiar. It's the boy Yoshi and I spoke to in the village. He made fun of me then, but he's not laughing now. His leg lies askew, and I can see it's badly broken.

"Don't worry," I say to his mother. "Ki-Yaga is a master of healing medicine. He set my broken arm, and now it is stronger than the other one."

The boy recognizes me, too. "Sorry," he whispers.

"It doesn't matter." I touch his shoulder gently to let him know I mean it.

He tries to smile, but it hurts too much.

"You're safe now," Mikko says. "Sensei is a wizard

with broken bones. Soon your leg will be so strong, you'll think it was magic."

"That's right. Sensei is so good, I trust him with my leg and I haven't got a spare one like you," I joke.

Laughter between friends is the best medicine. Sensei teaches us to brew herbs and set bones, but he also teaches us that humor heals the spirit. A samurai needs to be able to mend wounds of the body and mind. That's why a samurai does calligraphy and writes haiku as well as practices sword fighting and wrestling. The spirit needs exercise to stay healthy and happy.

Yoshi guides the stretcher bearers into the Healing Room. It's the same room where Sensei sleeps at night. In the middle is the healing table, crafted from the wood of the *ryu*'s first cherry tree. Bunches of herbs hang drying from the roof. Against the west wall is Sensei's hard bed with its thin cotton blanket.

"If my bed is too comfortable, I might never wake up," Sensei says. "I prefer to nap under a tree surrounded by the noise of practice. There, if I do not wake up in time, Niya will trip over me."

It's true. I fall over Sensei's long spidery legs all the

time. They're more lethal than my mother's goldfish bowls.

Kyoko and Sensei have dragged the table into the sun. Sensei believes in the healing power of sunlight. I do too. When the sun is warm against my back, my spirit soars and I am the White Crane, flying through summer.

The three villagers and Yoshi place the stretcher on the table. Riaze closes his eyes against the sun. He looks more peaceful already.

Sensei motions for everyone to leave, except the five of us and the boy's mother. He moves his hand gently along the broken leg, searching for fractures. His hands pause twice — two breaks need mending. The boy moans beneath the gentle pressure.

Taji sings a song about brave villagers defending their families from a dragon. Yoshi joins in, his deep, hypnotic voice weaving through the melody. Sensei hums. *Om. Om. Om.*

Riaze's whimpering softens, then stops. Kyoko takes a bamboo *shakuhachi,* a kind of flute, from her pocket and starts to play. Her notes pour over us in a cool waterfall of sound. Music takes you somewhere else, and it takes Riaze away from his pain. On outstretched wings, Kyoko's Zen flute flies where only Riaze and the White Crane can follow.

I know what my friends are doing. They're creating a distraction because the next bit is going to hurt, a lot. When I broke my arm, Sensei had to straighten it first. I can still hear myself scream. I wish I could find a way to help ease Riaze's pain, but I can't play the flute and my singing would ruin the song.

"If you can't find something, look in your heart. Many things get lost in there. It can take years for a memory to find its way out," Sensei says.

Looking inward, I see my sword. Taking Izuru from my belt, I place the hilt between Riaze's teeth.

"Here, bite on this. It will help."

Riaze gently bites into the leather as he slips his hand into mine. Sensei moves quickly. Suddenly, Riaze's sharp teeth clamp down hard, crushing the crane engraved on Izuru's handle. The White Crane cries

Riaze gently bites into the leather as
he slips his hand into mine.

inside my head as the teeth pierce his wing. Even with my sword in his mouth, Riaze screams. His body shakes as if an earthquake is rolling from head to toe.

"It's over now," I whisper, holding him still.

Sensei binds the leg firmly. Now the bone will heal properly and Riaze will walk and run through the village again. But first he must hop like me. That won't be easy for a two-legged boy.

Pling, pling! An idea blinks inside my brain. "Mikko, will you go and get the spare crutch from under my bed?"

Mikko nods and runs off. My extra crutch is special. Sensei helped me carve it from one of his favorite plum trees. He said he would not miss one tree when he has so many.

"I think you planted all these trees on purpose so you could spend your days sleeping and pretending to teach," I said.

Sensei raised one eyebrow. "Do you think I walked around as a young man planting trees for when I became old?"

I'm sure he did. One day I think I would like to be Sensei, sleeping in the sun.

"Maybe you will." The wizard's blazing blue eyes burrow into my head.

Mikko returns with the crutch, and I hand it to Riaze.

"Thank you. Now I am like you," he says.

"Another little frog hopper." Laughing at myself, I try to make him smile.

But Riaze doesn't laugh. "I am proud to be like you." He clutches my sword against his chest.

"You were very brave," Taji says.

Upset, the boy turns his face away. "I cried."

I understand how he feels. "Everyone cries. I cried louder than you did."

"You are kind. I am ashamed I made fun of you. Thank you for the crutch and the use of your sword."

"The sword is yours to keep." The words tumble out before I can stop them. I just gave away my best friend!

"No, no. I can't take it. I am not a samurai."

Sensei takes Riaze's hand. "Some samurai are born; others are made. This sword, Izuru, has your mark on it now. It distinguishes you as a samurai, because it was given from the heart of a samurai warrior. Next year, when your leg is strong, I will call for you, and your parents will decide if you can come to study with me."

Riaze is crying again but this time he is happy. Already I miss my sword, but I know it's time for me to say good-bye and let go of childhood weapons. Tomorrow I will have my *katana* and *wakizashi*.

Handing Riaze's mother two bags of herbs and a sac of *dokudami* wine, Sensei explains how to blend them to ease the pain. Poor Riaze. The cure is almost as bad as the broken leg. If he survives Sensei's wine, he's brave enough to be a samurai kid.

Riaze's mother gives Sensei a small sack of rice. She gives me an embarrassing hug. I smile politely and grit my teeth. She is so happy, she hugs us all. Even Sensei, who grits his teeth, too.

Sensei calls the villagers to take the boy home. Riaze is asleep now, my sword and crutch beside him. Despite her exhaustion, his mother lifts the stretcher's left corner. Love gives her great strength.

From Yoshi's rock, we watch them carefully track down the mountain.

"Why did you take her payment when we have plenty of rice?" Taji asks Sensei. "She is a poor woman." Taji doesn't miss anything. The soft sound of worn sandals and grains of rice rubbing together echoes like thunder in his ears.

"She needed to give it to me."

"Huh?" says Mikko.

"Sensei gave her dignity by accepting her payment for the service he provided," explains Kyoko.

Sensei nods. "It is important to serve. A samurai lives to serve. Sometimes what is right does not make immediate sense."

"Was it right for me to give him my sword?" I ask. It feels strange to be swordless. Without Izuru there is an empty space in my heart that even the White Crane cannot fill.

"Is it right for me to tell you what to do with your sword? What is right?" Sensei asks me in answer. It's the Zen thing, so I keep my mouth shut. NOTHING.

Later I ask a different question. "Why is Riaze coming to study with us? Once his leg is healed, there will be nothing wrong with him."

Sensei looks at me, teaching teeth bared in a smile.

"Do you think I chose you because you only had one leg? Foolish boy, I choose the best. I chose each of you because I saw great talent. It is not my problem if there are some other irrelevant parts missing. Now, after all my hard work in the sun, I would like a rest by the river. Swimming practice!"

The sun is high overhead, and the sweat drips down my neck into the folds of my kimono. You'd think I'd be happy to go swimming. I'm not. A samurai has to swim in his clothes and his armor. Wet clothes are heavy, and leather armor weighs a ton, even on dry land.

"No battle ever stopped so a warrior could put on his bathing suit," Sensei says.

"But we shouldn't put *more* clothes on to go swimming," says Yoshi. "We should take some off."

"We could go swimming in our underwear," suggests Mikko.

Sensei grins. "You cannot wield a sword if you are hiding embarrassed behind your hands. Kyoko would giggle so hard, she'd sink to the bottom."

Still complaining, we climb into our armor to go swimming.

The river runs through Uma's field, behind the kitchen. We file along the path with slow heavy steps. Uma nuzzles our empty pockets, searching for pudding. He stomps his foot to show his displeasure, and when Sensei offers him an apple, he snorts.

My eyes dart back and forth.

"I wouldn't worry about Black Tusk." Ki-Yaga smiles like the Sensei that swallowed the boar. He puts his fingers to his lips. "It's a surprise," he whispers.

It's not far to the river. A brisk five-minute walk, even in battle armor. I like the sound of water. When it rains, I lie in bed listening to the river race past. Water is restful and relaxing, as long as it is not in goldfish bowls on the floor.

Sensei has a favorite place where he likes to sleep and watch us swim. He closes his eyes and leans against the gnarled cherry tree.

I dive in with a clumsy *splash* and *splunk.* It's the best anyone can do, weighed down by leather. I kick hard with my one leg and I reach the middle, where no one can stand up, even if they have two feet.

Sensei opens one eye and his voice drifts out to teach me. "Different places have a way of leveling. What matters is where you stand, not how many legs you do it on."

I'm in the right place and ready for action. "Come on," I call. "Who wants a dunking?"

Kyoko swims over, her arms effortlessly carving up the water.

"Banzai!" she yells, pulling her practice sword from her sash and waving it in the air.

"Yah!" I answer, doing the same.

We touch sword points.

"One," Yoshi counts.

We turn and swim as fast as we can.

"Two, three. Turn," the others shout from the water's edge.

Kyoko and I double back and swim toward each other, swords raised. Then she disappears beneath the water. She pulls my one leg out from under me, and I sink, coughing and spluttering.

"Kyoko wins," Sensei calls. "When in the water, a samurai needs to keep an eye on what is below as well as what is above. There might be a river snake. Or worse, there might be a samurai girl."

Grumbling, I swim back to the edge with Kyoko. Next it's Mikko's turn to fight Taji.

Sensei's chest rises and falls with each snore.

"Shh." Kyoko puts her fingers to her lips. She pulls a bamboo ball of twine from her pocket, winks, and throws it at Taji's head. Taji's arm shoots straight out and catches it. Did he hear the ball in the air or Kyoko's wink? You can't sneak anything past the ears of a blind kid.

Laughing, Mikko ducks into the water, feet waving in the air. Taji times his throw perfectly. *Thwack.* Wet bamboo clunks Mikko on the foot. Taji roars and dives aside as Mikko aims at him.

Eventually we tire of being splatted in the head, feet, and backside.

"I'm hungry," I say, throwing my armor onto the riverbank beside Sensei. The others follow. Taji's armor lands with a wet thump in Sensei's lap. Teacher opens both eyes.

"I see I have been swimming too," he says, moving Taji's dripping armor aside. "Excellent. It must be time for lunch."

Inside the picnic basket I find fish and cucumber rolls, pickled ginger, and peaches. Yum. My stomach growls louder than Yoshi's Tiger.

We lie on the bank munching happily. Kyoko takes a napkin and twists and turns it. She's trying to make a cockroach again.

"If I can do this, I'll win an origami point at the Games."

But making a cockroach is hard. Only Sensei can do it.

"It's impossible," she complains.

"It is difficult," Sensei agrees. "Poor wretched me. I have five Little Cockroaches to finish."

He means us.

"If we are not finished, then what are we?" I ask.

"Bug bits. Cockroaches with pieces missing." Old eyes twinkle.

"Maybe I could slice off Kyoko's extra finger. That would be one bug finished," says Mikko, pretending to unsheathe his sword.

Kyoko throws a ball of paper at him. He dodges, and the ball flies into Sensei's hands. Twisting and folding, Sensei transforms the wrinkled imperfect page into a cockroach.

"It is amazing what I can make from things other people throw aside," he says.

He's talking about us again. I smile wider than my face. Lying in the sun, with a full stomach, I'm proud to be one of Sensei's bug bits.

CHAPTER EIGHT

真

GEMBUKU:
COMING OF AGE

Bang, Bang. Bang.

Sensei strides around our room banging his drum like a crazy man. He is crazy. Most mornings it's like this. We wake before the sun, and it's a struggle to open our eyes. It's easy for Sensei to get up in the morning, because he spends all day sleeping.

Still banging his drum, our master heads out the door toward the kitchen.

Today is a special day. Today we come of age. Instead of a boy's ponytail, we'll bind our long hair up like samurai men. I'll have two new blades: my *katana* and my *wakizashi*. When the Gembuku Ceremony is over, I'll be a warrior student.

I jump out of bed and stab at the bedclothes with an imaginary sword. The White Crane screeches to the others to wake. We throw on our kimonos, jackets, and trousers as fast as three layers of clothing will let us.

Summer mornings in the Tateyama Mountains are freezing cold. Steaming rice warms our bellies; breakfast readies us for the day ahead.

"Lots of work to do," Sensei announces. "We need to prepare for Gembuku."

Time has rushed through the *ryu*. With only two days until the tournament, we are still cockroaches fit for squashing.

"Today we paint our school," says Sensei.

"Ooooooh," I groan.

Once I helped Father paint. My arms ached; my leg ached. Painting isn't good practice for anything.

"We should be doing something special today, not yard work," I complain.

Sensei strokes his beard. "Niya has a good idea. We will do haiku."

Now everyone groans and glares at me. There's something worse than painting. Poetry! That's what haiku is. Haiku poems are only three lines long but hard to write. It's the worst class in samurai school.

When I was younger, I thought haiku was an even greater punishment. It sounds like *seppuku,* when a samurai warrior slits his stomach open to save himself from dishonor. Lucky for us, the custom isn't practiced any more. After our performance at the last Samurai Trainee Games, we would all be gutless. Still, writing haiku is almost as painful as emptying the contents of your stomach.

Sensei recites a poem.

Ten thousand words.
Snake tongue flickers.
The sword falls.

"Who would like to comment?" he asks.

I suppose the only decent poem is one with a sword in it. "I agree with the guy who chopped the head off the snake," I volunteer.

Kyoko giggles, so I know I've got it wrong.

"There is no snake in this poem," says Sensei. "Become blind. Close your eyes to the words, and open your heart to the images."

I close my eyes, and the words disappear. It's a good start. No more poem! I try hard, but I don't understand. I think about the sword. Chop. Chop. The White Crane swings its razor-sharp beak, and the water snake falls in pieces.

"A word on a sharp tongue is a lethal as a sword," says Taji. He has an unfair advantage. He doesn't have to try to become blind.

"A true samurai doesn't need a sword," adds Yoshi. Sensei nods, pleased.

The burble of their voices washes over me. Closing my eyes, I give up on haiku and let the White Crane fly while the others do more poems.

Thwreck-creck! A crack of thunder reminds me to return to land.

Sensei claps his hands again. "Now we will paint," he says.

"Hoy. Hoy-hoy," a voice calls from the practice compound. It's Onaku. We're saved by the swordsmith and his beautiful wife.

Yoshi runs to take the harness from Onaku's back. Strong as an ox, the Sword Master carried all our weapons up the mountain. He lays two large packages on a blanket under the cherry tree.

Mrs. Onaku has a package too: yellow silk tied with

ribbons of straw. She gives it to Kyoko, and they undo it together. New kimonos!

We always wear cockroach brown. A samurai should attract attention with his sword, not his clothes. But there's nothing drab about our new brown kimonos; they shine like bronzed earth. A Dragon would be proud to wear one.

Mrs. Onaku whispers in Kyoko's ear, and they both giggle.

"What?" I ask.

"Girl talk." Kyoko giggles again.

The Snow Monkey is a trickster spirit. One day Kyoko climbed Sensei's plum tree and pelted us with fruit.

"Get down!" we called.

"Stop it!" bellowed Mikko.

But Kyoko laughed at us, a big samurai belly laugh, not a girlish giggle. "I am the Snow Monkey," she called, shaking her white hair. "I climb trees to throw things at pesky bats and birds."

When Sensei saw our plum-stained clothes, he made

us go down to the river and wash them. Kyoko came to help, still laughing. The laughter of a friend doesn't hurt. It tickles until you begin to laugh, too.

Onaku undoes the first of his packages. No one speaks. Six swords lie on the blanket. I recognize mine, with the White Crane dancing around its handle. My heart stops for a second, and in the dead silence, the sword sings to me.

The Sword Master gestures to Yoshi to open the second package. Six *wakizashi* blades gleam in the sun.

"Why are there six swords and daggers?" Mikko asks. "There are only five of us."

Sensei's eyes smile. "You never know when you might need a spare set."

I can't imagine that Onaku's fine swords would ever break. Some men pay a year's wages for a weapon with his signature on the hilt. But the Sword Master will not let Sensei pay.

"It is not honorable for a samurai to deal in silver and gold. I respect that," Onaku says.

"Even the Sword Master must eat," Sensei replies.

"I do not eat silver and gold."

"Good," says Sensei. "Because I do not have either. Have a flask of *dokudami* wine instead."

"I'll take two. They're very good swords." Onaku guffaws and pats his large belly.

The two old friends tell the same stories all the time, sharing the shade under the cherry tree. Sensei crosses his chopstick-thin legs and tucks his beard into his belt. Onaku squats on trunk-thick legs and scratches his bald head.

We try to get them to talk about the samurai kids who studied at the Cockroach Ryu in the old days, before we came. I like to hear about Mitsuka Manuyoto. His name is carved in the wood above my pillow. He's an old man now, living as a hermit somewhere by the ocean. But once he was a samurai kid like me and slept in my bed.

"Mitsuka was a great warrior," Onaku begins. "His skills were famous far and wide. He went to serve the Emperor." Pausing, the Sword Master scratches behind his ear. "I seem to remember Mitsuka wasn't a good horseman. He was always falling off. In fact, Mitsuka was the clumsiest kid I'd ever seen. He kept dropping his sword. I had to make him a special one with a sticky grip on the hilt."

"All my students have something to overcome. It leads them to great things," says Sensei.

Onaku nods. "Mitsuka grew into greatness under your master's teaching. When Mitsuka raised his sword, it was like lightning in his fingers. Single-handedly, he protected the Emperor from six ninja assassins. He became a national hero, and the Emperor declared him a Japanese treasure."

I remember seeing Mitsuka when I was young. Mother and Father took me to the ceremony where the Emperor rewarded his samurai bravery.

Onaku continues with his story. "'Thank you,' the Emperor said, kneeling before his defender.

"'No. I am your servant.' Mitsuka helped the Emperor to his feet. *'Chi. Jin. Yu.'*

"'You are well trained, Samurai Warrior,' the Emperor said.

"'My teacher was the great Ki-Yaga.' Mitsuka bowed.

"The Emperor hesitated for just a moment. 'I thought he was dead.'"

Onaku laughs at his own telling, and we all join in.

"Enough stories," declares Sensei. "It is time. Gembuku has come."

Mrs. Onaku has a razor in her hand. I reach up and run my fingers through my long, dark strands. I will never look or feel the same again. I am about to become a man.

"Who's first?" she asks.

"Me," volunteers Taji.

She undoes Taji's ponytail. Jet-black hair gleams in the sun as she shaves a strip on each side of his head. Then Mrs. Onaku reties the ponytail and winds it into a knot, pinned with a bamboo clip.

"How do I look?" Taji asks. It's important to answer right. Taji will never see his transformation into a samurai warrior, except through our eyes.

"You look older," I say.

"You look brave," Yoshi says.

"And honorable," says Mikko.

Taji smiles, pleased.

"You look handsome," says Kyoko.

He turns bright red, but he's still smiling.

Mrs. Onaku finishes the boys first. Looking at my reflection in the mirror, I see that I am older, brave, and honorable, too. And handsome. The White Crane preens its feathers.

Last it's Kyoko's turn. Pale hair falls onto the pile of black, like powdery snow on rock. But there's nothing gentle about a samurai girl. The bruise on my arm from wrestling Kyoko yesterday throbs when I touch it.

We follow Mrs. Onaku to our room to change into our new kimonos. While Kyoko disappears behind her screen to dress, we struggle with the wraps and ties. At least it's only one layer. For special occasions we just wear our kimonos.

At Gembuku, students in less old-fashioned *ryu* get a new name. Not us. Sensei says sometimes the old ways have to give way to the new, and sometimes new and old have to live together.

"You will not be a new person, so you do not need a new name. You were samurai long before a sword told you so," says Sensei. "It is hard enough for me to remember the names of all my students, without giving them new ones halfway through their studies."

Ba-boom. Boom. Boom. The ceremonial gong in the practice area sounds. It rang on the day we came to the *ryu,* when Sensei called us for the first time. Now it rings as we join together to come of age.

Mrs. Onaku leads us, single file, to where Sensei and the Sword Master are waiting. Our weapons are laid out on a long, low table. Another covered table sits under Sensei's favorite plum tree.

Kneeling in a row in front of the swords, we wait for the ceremony to begin. Onaku stands behind the gong with Sensei beside him and Mrs. Onaku sitting at the table's end.

Ba-boom! Onaku strikes the gong. Sound echoes across the valley. Everyone in the mountains will hear it and know that Gembuku has come to the Cockroach Ryu.

Sensei calls my name: "Student Niya Moto." Without my crutch, I hop toward him. Today I do not care how many legs are missing. Standing in front of my master, I am proud of who I am.

Onaku hands Sensei my sword. I kneel, and he taps me gently on one shoulder. As I rise, he holds out my *katana*.

When I touch the handle, the sword sings so loudly that my fingers falter. The blade falls through my hand, clattering into the dust. Silence crushes my chest hard. I can barely breathe. I wish the ground would open and an earthquake would swallow me. I wish Yoshi had left me on the mountainside.

Laughing, Onaku slaps me on the back.

"Just like Mitsuka. You're going to be a great samurai warrior, young Niya." He picks up the sword and passes it to me. "No wonder this sword sang so strong. It is in good hands."

"Thank you," I say, glad to be breathing again.

"Nothing ever goes according to plan," counsels Sensei. "Best not to expect it to and plan nothing. Remember this lesson."

"I remember NOTHING," I say. Then I do something unplanned, just as Sensei taught me. Raising my sword high, I call to the White Crane. "Ay-ee-ah!" I jump high and kick, landing perfectly on one foot.

"I am pleased with your progress, student."

"I am pleased with your progress, student." Sensei bows to show his respect. "You are now a novice samurai warrior, having traveled halfway along the path. Bushido go with you as you continue on your way." He takes the dagger and hands it to me. I grasp it firmly and tuck it safely into my belt. Kneeling again, I bend my forehead to the dirt. "Master," I say.

"Rise, samurai." Sensei's eyes shine with pride.

Leaving my childhood behind, I return to my place beside Yoshi. I am still Niya. Sensei was right. I don't need a new name.

Finally we all have our swords and daggers.

"Now, my Little Cockroaches, let us eat," Sensei proclaims.

Mrs. Onaku uncovers the second table and reveals the ceremonial last meal of a samurai. Just as we left one life behind when we came to study with Sensei, we are now dead to our childhood. The table is set with dried chestnuts, kelp, and abalone. There is *sake* in red lacquered drinking cups. But there's one extra smell. Something new. Roast pig! It's Black Tusk. He won't be bothering us again.

"Why do you still call us Little Cockroaches?" I ask. "We have grown older today."

"Do you feel any bigger?" asks Sensei.

"No," I admit.

"That's because you are still little." Bacon grease dribbles down Sensei's chin, and he wipes it with his cloak. "But you are much wiser. What is it you have learned?"

Teacher sits cross-legged, waiting for pearls of wisdom to drop in his lap.

"If you are chased by a boar, run fast," says Yoshi. *Clink.* The first pearl.

"Run very fast," Taji elaborates.

Kyoko grins. "A true samurai doesn't need a sword."

"Not if he can yell loud." I think of Sensei, weaponless as he screeched in to attack the boar.

"The point of the sword is very sharp," Mikko says.

Clink, clink, clink. Sensei's lap is full.

"I am such a good teacher. I think I deserve a nap." Leaning back against his tree, our master closes his eyes.

Onaku looks at us and winks. "Let's go fishing. Maybe I can poach some fish out of your river before Ki-Yaga catches me."

We leave Sensei to snore and Mrs. Onaku to clear away the lunch. Grinning, the Sword Master produces a fishing rod from under his ceremonial cloak. He planned this all along!

As we pass the kitchen, I sneak a dollop of pudding for Uma. Our horse gallops to meet me, licking my fingers until every honeyed rice grain is gone. Then he walks beside us to the river.

"Do you think we should have left Sensei behind?" I ask.

"Do you think he would have let us, if he did not want us to go?" answers Onaku.

He's right. Even asleep, Sensei is wide awake.

Kyoko pulls at the pin in my topknot. "How long have you known our teacher?" she asks Onaku, ducking behind Uma so I can't retaliate.

"Since I was a boy."

"What was Sensei like as a boy?" Taji wants to know.

The swordsmith shakes his head. "Ki-Yaga wasn't

a boy. He was old even then. He chooses his students carefully. Few are chosen. In the years when he had no students, he came to the village to teach and tell stories. I always pushed my way to the front, to sit and listen at his feet. As I grew older, we became friends. I helped him build the *ryu*."

"But the *ryu* is very old," Mikko says.

"Only the trees. Your teacher planted trees long before the school was built. He doesn't care to look after the buildings, but he cares about trees. Ki-Yaga is older than the forest and wiser than the mountain."

"Why didn't you become a samurai?" I ask. "I'm sure Sensei would have taught you."

"Did you ever want to become a swordsmith?"

"No. I've always wanted to be a samurai. It's in my heart."

"It was like that for me. The swords were calling, even when I was a boy. But now"—Onaku grins—"the fish are yelling."

I like fish. Even the goldfish in Mother's bowls that flop out to trip me. Even the ones that swim in my stomach when I am nervous. Best of all, I like raw fish on my dinner plate, wrapped in seaweed and dipped in soy sauce. Sushi. Yum. My mouth waters, and the White Crane snaps its beak.

But catching fish is boring. Leaning against Sensei's tree, Onaku doesn't notice. He sleeps while the fish gobble his bait.

"Let's practice," suggests Taji. We can use our new swords."

Now that we've come of age, we're allowed to practice with real swords. Sensei still prefers us to use our wooden ones. But we have to use the new ones at the Samurai Trainee Games this year. It can't hurt to try them out now. "I'll go first," I say. I want to test mine and Taji is easy to beat.

"I see you," he calls as he raises his blade.

I'm sure he can't. I'm standing very still. There's nothing for Taji to hear.

You should never underestimate the ears of a blind samurai kid. The flat part of Taji's blade whacks me across the nose and squashes it flat as a sheet of rice paper. Again.

"Sorry, Ni," he apologizes.

"Good shot," I snort. "I'll get you later."

I was wrong. It *does* hurt to use our new swords. Yoshi's loud chuckle echoes across the mountains.

Onaku wakes with a jolt and surveys my bloody face.

"Not the first time that's happened, Niya?" he asks me.

Rolling my eyes, I shake my head.

"We'll go back and get Ki-Yaga to look at it," Onaku decides.

"Not again," Sensei says as he packs my nose in ice. Later he binds it with yellow tape. The White Crane looks like a vulture.

CHAPTER NINE

仁

RAT BOY

We wait in a line while Sensei inspects our packing for the journey. It'll take us two days to walk to the Games, and we have to carry everything we need—food, clothing, and our equipment.

"Good. Almost complete," he says.

"What have we missed?" I memorized the list and checked it twice. I'm sure I haven't forgotten anything.

"You need rain cloaks."

Mikko raises his eyebrows at me. The sky is clear and blue. It's been cloudless for weeks.

"Are you sure it's going to rain, Sensei?" Taji asks.

"If we had a boat, I would suggest you take it."

We rush off to get our cloaks. When we return, Sensei is standing in the drizzle, drops falling from his pointy nose to form puddles around his sandals. Uma is waiting also, his tail flicking water at anyone who stands too close.

134

"This year you are warrior students, and your Games' team needs a captain. I have chosen Yoshi," Sensei announces.

Yoshi was born to lead. He's always carried more on his shoulders than the rest of us, and I'm not talking about harnesses and packages. Ever since that day on the mountain, I'd follow Yoshi anywhere. Even to the Games and back.

We leave together, but Sensei and Uma travel a different way. Sensei says it's good for us to travel without him. He says it makes us think instead of using his brain. We'll take a shortcut through the tunnel between this peak and the next. Horses don't like tunnels, so Sensei and Uma will go the long way around, down one mountain and up the other. But Sensei will still get there first.

It's not because he rides. He doesn't. Sensei has a pack strapped to his back.

"Uma is a warrior, not a packhorse," he says.

Sensei is stronger than a horse anyway. Our master will get there first because he walks very fast, with long, spidery wizard steps with which only Uma can keep up.

"I will give you a half day's head start," Sensei decides. "I don't want to be waiting too long at the other end. I might fall asleep."

I'm sure he will. Anywhere he can find a cherry tree.

The old village woman's words seep through my thoughts. Maybe Sensei doesn't walk. Maybe he flies. A black *tengu* crow wings across my imagination and off into the distance. As I shake the image from my head, my topknot unravels and I slap myself in the face with my soggy ponytail. That'll teach me to daydream.

Waving to Sensei, we begin the trek to the tunnel mouth. Our mountain is named Oyama. The mountain we are walking to is called Tsurugidake, "Sword Mountain," because it's shaped like a sword. At the top of Mount Tsurugidake is the Temple of the Komusu, the Priests of Emptiness and Nothingness. And some of the best swordsmen in the world!

Komusu priests were samurai in their younger days, but now they have set aside their blades for flutes, which are just as lethal. They are carved from the root of a bamboo, and their tapered ends are as sharp as swords and capable of killing an opponent. The point of the flute is very sharp. Sensei's words twist and turn in my brain.

Old people, like my grandfather, say the Komusu flute bewitches the soul with its ghostly Zen tones. It's difficult to play, but when Kyoko's six fingers dance over five holes, my soul soars and the White Crane flies higher than ever.

The Komusu are as old as Sensei. They wear baskets over their heads to show that they're separate from the world they no longer want to see. The priests rarely speak, except for the four eldest, when they oversee the Games. Even then, their sentences are short and their voices raspy from a year of wordlessness.

"I'm going to join the Komusu when I get old. I like the idea of sitting in silence. You might like it too, Kyoko. You're good with a flute," Taji says.

"What? Wear a basket on my head? Still, it might be an improvement for you," she says with a laugh.

We work our way down the familiar path. This is our third Games. We know the way well enough to walk it in the dark. Like Taji does.

The path is muddy and slippery, and the sky grows gloomier with each step. By the middle of the afternoon, day looks like night.

"We should tell stories," says Mikko. "It'll give us something to do."

I agree. The Komusu might like the sound of silence, but I prefer the chatter of conversation. It's miserable walking in the rain. My sandals are wet and uncomfortable, and we have a long way to go.

"I'll start," begins Kyoko. "Once upon a time, there was a beautiful princess growing inside a bamboo stalk. Bamboo Spirit found her and looked after her. Then one day the princess disappeared. The bamboo was so sad that it grew and grew until it filled the forests with sorrow. That's why you find bamboo growing everywhere."

"What a terrible story. Bor-ring," Mikko moans.

Taji makes kissy noises. "Girls' stuff."

"Have you got a better one?" Kyoko retorts.

Mikko nods. "I'll tell you about my favorite monster."

"Which one?" asks Yoshi.

"Guess. It's huge, fanged, and horned like a bull. Capable of dark magic. If you chop its arm off, it grows another one."

"No wonder you like it," Kyoko says with a giggle. "You need another arm."

Mikko's one arm is doubly strong. He swings it hard at Kyoko. But it's not easy to scare a samurai girl. Dodging, Kyoko makes a face, and Mikko smiles.

"Shh. I want to hear," I say. "Monster stories are better than tales about princesses."

Sticking out her tongue, Kyoko pokes me in the arm. It hurts.

"The *oni* carries a large, spiky iron bar. It walks the earth from hell"—Mikko's voice drops to an ominous whisper—"and it eats human flesh."

Lightning splits the sky and illuminates our frightened faces. We trudge through the rain and imagine monsters waiting to jump out and eat us. Another sword thrust of lightning strikes the earth in front of Yoshi, forcing us to shelter in a rock alcove.

"I'll tell a story now. About the *kappa,* the water

spirit, a giant deformed turtle," Taji says. "Like me, it likes to wrestle. If you lose when it challenges you, it will steal your stomach."

"Watch out, Niya." Yoshi chortles. "You could never survive without your stomach." Everyone laughs. Friendly laughter, not like the ridicule waiting for me at the Games.

"The *kappa* is very strong," Taji continues, "but it needs to keep its head wet or it'll die. It likes rain. The *kappa* is out walking this path tonight." He pauses. "Maybe it's sneaking up now. . . ."

I shiver. I think I can hear something.

"Raa!" Taji yells. We all jump up screaming.

Taji shakes with mirth until Kyoko gives him a shove. In the slap of rain on rock, his ears miss the cue and he goes sprawling out into the mud. Taji grabs at Kyoko as he falls and she catches her foot in mine. I stumble headfirst into Yoshi. Only Mikko escapes.

"Make room for me." He grins and slides into the sludge. We roll around, throwing handfuls at each other until we look like swamp monsters.

We form a muddy, soaked line to follow
our leader through the rain.

"Time to go," Yoshi says, wiping his eyes and smearing dirt across his cheeks.

We form a muddy, soaked line to follow our leader through the rain. An hour passes slowly.

Splat! A wet branch smacks me in the face. I'm tired of tramping though the dripping forest. The rain has stopped, but droplets of water still plop from the trees onto my head. My sandals squelch, and my toes squish. Wet trousers slap at my ankles.

The White Crane's feathers are sodden clumps. Striped Gecko wants a rock in the sun, and the Golden Bat and Snow Monkey huddle against each other. The Tiger is a drowned kitten. With each saturated step, our spirits sink lower. One foot after another, we follow Yoshi through the sludge.

He stops suddenly. I smack into the back of him, and Taji falls over me. Down go Kyoko and Mikko. Into the mud we tumble, again.

Yoshi's Tiger nose sniffs the air. "I smell a rat."

"How big?" Mikko's one hand is on his sword as he searches the undergrowth.

"Monster big," says Yoshi.

"Can you see anything, Taji?" Kyoko asks.

It's not a stupid question. Sometimes Taji sees better than all of us, especially when we don't know what we are looking for.

"Two eyes are a great handicap when you are searching for something," Sensei says. "It is hard to see past all the distractions. But the blind man sees with his nose and ears. He sees much clearer."

"It's over there." Taji indicates, pointing to a thick bamboo clump.

Yoshi sniffs and nods.

Sword drawn, Mikko rushes over. He pokes through the stalks but finds nothing.

"It's gone," he says.

"Well, I'm starving. Let's stop and eat," suggests Yoshi.

We're all tired and hungry, glad to take our heavy bundles from our backs. Yoshi props the extra sword and dagger against the stand of bamboo. After rice cakes and plum juice, I close my eyes and pretend I am Sensei dozing against a cherry tree in the sun. But my students will not let me rest. Kyoko tickles my toes until I open my eyes. Yoshi's nose is twitching again. Taji swings around, his blind eyes staring into the bamboo.

Suddenly a scrawny hand wraps around the spare *katana* handle. The remainder of the thief's body is hidden behind the thick stalks.

Mikko unsheathes his blade.

"Put that down, or I'll slice your hand off," he threatens.

Slech. The *katana* drops with a sloppy thud.

"Come out," commands Yoshi.

A thin, grubby boy edges out from behind the bamboo. His nose is long and narrow like a rat; his hands and feet are black with mud. He's almost as dirty as us.

Silence falls like a guillotine. The boy touched a samurai sword. The penalty is death. We never questioned the rules in the classroom at the *ryu.* But here on the mountain, we don't like them anymore. No one wants to kill this boy.

"What are we going to do?" whispers Kyoko.

Rat Boy says nothing. Black rodent eyes dart from one face to another.

"Maybe we could just teach him a lesson," says Mikko.

Kyoko shakes her head. "The rules say he has to die."

"We don't have to obey the rules," Yoshi declares. We all look surprised. Yoshi never breaks the rules. "Sensei taught us sometimes the old ways have to change," he explains.

We're all relieved with Yoshi's decision. Especially Rat Boy. Sensei chose our leader well.

"He might be a samurai. How do we know he's not a samurai?" I ask.

"He doesn't look like one," Mikko says.

"Do we look like samurai?" Taji laughs. Who ever heard of a one-armed swordsman or a one-legged warrior? Or a blind archer?

"Maybe it's *his*," I say. "Sensei was insistent about us bringing the extra sword. Maybe the boy is the rightful owner."

Everyone likes my idea. Yoshi nods approval, and Mikko hands the sword to the Rat Boy.

He's looking at Mikko. As if he recognizes him.

Mikko looks at Rat Boy. Now there's recognition in his eyes, too.

"This is Nezume. He's a samurai kid, all right," Mikko says. "He's a Dragon."

Silence falls again. A Dragon! We just gave one of our swords to a Dragon kid.

"He's one of the boys who cut off my arm."

You wouldn't think the silence could get any bigger, but it does. We just gave one of Onaku's prized swords to a cheat and bully.

"Maybe he *should* die," says Mikko.

I know he doesn't mean it. "A life for an arm seems unfair. Perhaps we should cut off his arm," I suggest. "Then he'd be the same as you."

"And he was only one of three. We would have to cut off one-third," Kyoko calculates.

"Bushido is the answer," I say. "*Chi, jin, yu. Jin* for benevolence and kindness."

Everyone nods, including Mikko. We want to be benevolent. No one wants to hurt Nezume. Or cut off his arm. Not even his finger.

"Perhaps he should say something. He's got his own

tongue. Unless someone chopped that off. Would you like to say something?" Yoshi asks the Dragon boy.

"I want to tell Mikko I'm sorry," says Nezume. "Because I was frightened, I did what the bigger boys told me. But after Mikko left, I ran away. I didn't want to be a samurai kid anymore. For three years I have hidden in the forest. Each time I saw Mikko pass by, I wanted to apologize. But I was too ashamed to speak. I am not worthy of any sword."

"Yes, you are," decides Mikko. "Like me, you're not a Dragon anymore."

"A new sword has chosen you. You're a Cockroach now. Would you like to come with us to the Games?" Yoshi asks.

"Please do," pleads Kyoko.

It's hard to refuse Kyoko, but Nezume looks at Mikko and hesitates.

"We want you to come with us. We all do." Mikko smiles. *Jin* for benevolence and the beginning of a friendship.

"You have to come," I say. "Our sensei is expecting you. Ki-Yaga chose you to join us. Why else would he have made us carry an extra sword and dagger across the Tateyama Mountains?"

"Then I have no choice . . ." Nezume's voice trails off.

"Good. But if you are still feeling guilty, you can carry my pack," says Mikko.

We all laugh. Even Nezume.

"Hey, it's stopped raining." Kyoko cups six fingers skyward.

Yoshi hoists the harness onto his back, signaling that it's time to resume traveling. *Caw. Caw.* A black crow wings overhead, disappearing into the mountain forest.

"There goes Sensei," jokes Mikko, waving into the distance.

Nezume gasps and shakes his head. "You mustn't make fun of the mountain spirit."

"Why not?" says Taji. "It's just a story."

"No! No!" Nezume shakes his head harder than before. "The *tengu* are real. I met one once."

The White Crane turns a black beady eye to study Nezume's face. Honesty stares back.

"Did he have a snowy beard down to his knees? And a long, skinny nose?" I describe Sensei.

"He was tall and thin, with a dark tattered cloak, but I didn't see a beard. He taught me how to survive in the mountains and said I was welcome to stay while I waited for my friends. I thought I would be here forever because I have no friends. No one wants me."

"We understand. Before Sensei, no one wanted us, either," says Yoshi.

"We're your friends." Kyoko hugs Nezume. Only a samurai girl can wield a hug like a weapon. There's no arguing against Kyoko's arms. And they feel good, too.

"Maybe the old man was Sensei in disguise. Maybe he hid his beard. That's an easy trick for a wizard," I muse.

Mikko rolls his eyes. "I think there's rainwater in your brain."

"Ki-Yaga could be a *tengu*," says Nezume. "If all the stories about him are true."

They are. Sensei is wise beyond this world.

"But a *tengu* is a samurai who has fallen from grace," reminds Kyoko. "Sensei doesn't make mistakes, he's perfect."

"We all make mistakes, even when we don't mean to," says Nezume, thinking of himself.

"Yes," agrees Yoshi. "I don't think Sensei is a *tengu*, but I know mistakes are easily made and can't be undone." In Yoshi's memory, his friend is rolling down the hill.

The rain begins again.

"I know a shortcut to the tunnel," Nezume volunteers.

"Let's take it," says Taji. "I don't want to drip all the way to the temple."

Leading us away from the path, Nezume weaves under large flat-leaf plants and pushes through dense stands of bamboo. Before long, the tunnel gapes ahead. Sensei told us it was carved out by a river running through a fissure in the rock. A drip of water can carve through a mountain, given time.

Maybe. I haven't got that long to wait for anything. A samurai does his carving with his *katana*.

Inside the mountain smells like rain and moldy old

age. Taji likes it here. The Golden Bat is happy in the gloom, but I don't like being under the earth. I don't trust it.

We are soon surrounded by stone. With arms only half outstretched, I can touch both sides of the damp walls. Even the sky has turned to rock, hanging low and threatening above my head. Everything is brown and black. The light at the end of this tunnel is hours away.

A cockroach should feel at home here, but I prefer open space and fresh air. If we hurry, we'll be out of the tunnel by sunset. Kyoko lights a tree-wax candle and hands it to Yoshi. The tunnel will grow darker with each step toward the center.

Quickly, we make our way along the passages and through the caves. For centuries, the samurai and priests of the mountains have traveled this way. The walls are narrow in places and crowd Yoshi's wide shoulders. Sometimes we have to climb under rocks jutting from the ceiling. But most of the way we can walk side by side.

Suddenly, when we are only halfway through, the tunnel fills with sound. Wet. Roaring. It's not an earthquake. It's a new danger.

"Hang on to something. Grab anything. Quick!" Nezume yells over the roar.

There's not much to choose from. I cling to a straggly plant rooted in the cave wall. Beside me, Mikko grabs a protruding stone. Taji is pinned flat against the rock face.

A river of mud comes sliding down the narrow stretch of tunnel. My foot is knocked from under me, and my hand slips.

"Niya!" I hear Mikko call. Someone else is screaming. Kyoko, I think.

Struggling, the White Crane tries to swim. Mud fills my mouth. I open it to spit out the sludge, but more comes rushing in. It's freezing cold. Mud pushes into my nostrils. I'm glad when the ooze seeps into my brain and I can't feel anything anymore.

CHAPTER TEN

NEZUME'S WAY

I dream Kyoko is kissing me. I never thought about that before. It feels good and warm, so I decide to stay asleep and never wake up. But someone won't let me. Someone is shaking me hard.

When I open my eyes, Yoshi is leaning over me, his face close to mine.

"Yech," I splutter. I don't want to kiss Yoshi.

"He's alive!" Taji whoops, his voice echoing off the cave walls.

Yoshi flips me over like a rag doll and belts me on the back. Spluttering and coughing, I empty the contents of my stomach at his feet.

"We thought you were dead," Nezume says.

I might be yet. Kyoko threatens to suffocate me with her embrace.

"I wasn't going to lie there with Yoshi kissing me.

Blech," I croak, my throat dry and sore from swallowing mud.

"We all had a turn." Mikko laughs. "You're a terrible kisser."

Pffut! Making a face, I blow a raspberry at him, but in my heart the White Crane knows it is lucky to have friends like these.

The candle spits and spatters. I scoop lumps of mud out of my ear and sneeze to clear my nostrils.

"We need to keep moving," Yoshi says. "We don't want to miss the Games' Opening Ceremony."

Nervously, I look along the tunnel behind me. I'm more worried about the mountain sliding again.

Kyoko rummages in her backpack, a look of panic spreading across her face. "There're no more candles. They must have fallen out when I slipped in the mud."

"Then we have to walk faster than one candle," decides Yoshi. "Are you ready to go, Niya?"

"Don't worry about me. I could run if I had two legs," I say, shaking my brain to clear the sludge. My head thumps as if Sensei is banging his drum inside it, and my ear echoes with the *drip, drip* of imaginary water.

But it's not me we need to worry about. As Mikko rises, his foot slips. *Thwack.* He lands with a wet crunch, the slap of bone against rock.

"Let me try that again," he says, and grins. His smile fades as he collapses, clutching his ankle.

"Let me have a look." Taji searches with his fingers, the way Sensei did with Riaze's leg. This time the news is good. Mikko grunts and groans, but he doesn't yell.

"It's only sprained," Taji says.

With Nezume's help, Mikko struggles to stand. "I don't think I'm going to be able to walk very fast."

It's important to heal the spirit, too. I've had a lot of practice teasing Mikko, so I know exactly what to say. "Whining won't get you any sympathy from me. I have to hop around all the time."

Mikko's spirit rises to the challenge. "I should get rice bags full of sympathy. Now I've got one arm and one leg." He swings a playful punch, then lunges for Taji instead. Luckily, Taji hears and ducks out of the way, but Mikko lands in the mud again.

I grin. For once I'm not the only one-legged samurai kid in Japan. There's another one, even clumsier than me.

"Let's go." Yoshi moves first. Kyoko puts one hand in his. The other holds onto Nezume, with Mikko leaning on his shoulder. Then Taji. Then me. We stretch out like a row of paper people, the kind we sometimes make in origami class when Sensei's not looking. Ki-Yaga teaches us that to know a man, you must walk in his shoes, but I think you learn even more when you hold someone's hand.

Together we slosh and slap through the mud until it rises to suck at our ankles. We wade through knee-deep sludge, kicking aside stones and upended plants in our haste. Lengths of kudzu vine tangle around our legs. In my imagination, mud monsters drag me under again. Their tendril grip tightens across my ankles.

Many years ago, Gaiya, the old Eagle Sensei, walked into the mountain and never came out. Sensei told us the story in the year we first traveled to the Games.

"That's awful," Kyoko said.

"What happened?" Taji wanted to know.

"He found peace and decided to stay," Sensei answered.

But the kids from the Eagle Ryu tell a different story. They say Gaiya's spirit flies lost in the tunnel and if you listen carefully, you can hear his shadowy wings. I'm not afraid of ghosts, but I rest my hand on my sword. Just in case.

With each step, the air grows colder, the walls move closer, and the ceiling drops to sometimes scrape Yoshi's head. We're walking single file now.

"Not much farther." Nezume's words of encouragement freeze in the air.

"G-good," stutters Kyoko. "I've got ice-block feet."

My teeth chatter. "Me, too."

Suddenly Yoshi stops. I crash into Taji, knocking him against Mikko. One by one, we stumble and fall over. But Yoshi stands firm. He has to. There's nothing in front of him except a yawning black hole. A great chunk of the path is missing. For three times the length of my crutch, there's no floor at all.

"What do we do now?" Mikko asks.

"Niya will think of something," Yoshi says. "He's good at problem solving."

I wish I had an answer. With its wings wet and mud-heavy, even the White Crane can't fly over this chasm. I'm worried, too. This is not our first trip through the tunnel. The way is sometimes narrow, sometimes steep, and often slippery, but it has always been safe. Now the mountain is moving again, shifting and rearranging. How can I find a path through thin air?

Here the tunnel is two kids wide. On one side, the wall drops sheer into the jagged fissure. On the other side is a narrow ledge, just wide enough for one foot. But if we slip . . .

The path has collapsed into such a dark pit, even the White Crane can't see where it ends.

The vine unwraps itself from my ankle and tugs at my brain. "I've got an idea."

Yoshi doesn't look surprised. "I knew you would work it out."

"We could make a rope harness from the kudzu and tie it around our waists," I suggest. "It won't stop us from falling, but at least we won't hit the bottom."

Yoshi nods. "Excellent. If we feel safe, we'll take confident steps."

His praise makes me feel less nervous already.

Kyoko claps her hands. "I'm the best climber. I'll go first and anchor the rope on the other side. I'll throw the end back for the next person."

Kyoko can climb anything, even the *ryu* flagpole. The pole is thin and smooth, taller than Sensei's cherry trees, but she runs up it faster than the flag.

But there's still a problem. A safety harness might make us feel better, but it doesn't make the ledge any easier to cross. If we lose our footing, we'll plunge into the crevice and swing into the rock face on the other side. Still, being flattened against a rock is better than being broken into pieces at the bottom of a pit.

"I'll go next," volunteers Nezume. "I'm not afraid of heights."

He's also very brave.

"There comes a time when every life hangs by a thread," Sensei once said.

"Yes, Master," I answered, thinking I understood. But I never pictured it like this, tied to the end of a vine.

"Mikko follows Nezume," says Yoshi, sorting us by weight and strength until we all belong somewhere.

Yoshi goes last because he's our leader and a good captain steers from behind. Anyone can lead from the front.

Expert at finding things in the dark, Taji quickly pulls vines from under the mud. Kyoko weaves the strands into a thick rope. It's up to me to calculate the length. Too much will be heavy for Kyoko to carry, and too little won't reach back to us.

"How long is a piece of string?" Sensei often challenges. I never know. But I know how long a vine harness needs to be.

"We've got enough now," I decide.

Kyoko knots the end and places loops of rope around her waist.

"You are the Snow Monkey," Yoshi says. "You were born to climb across mountains."

I wish I were blind like Taji so I didn't have to look. But Kyoko doesn't hesitate. She's climbing the flagpole sideways until with a wet squelch, she lands on the other side.

Our *hurrah*s echo up and down the tunnel.

Kyoko wraps the rope around a large rock and ties it tight. She kicks the rock to check that it holds firm. It's a good test because Kyoko kicks harder than all of us. I know. I've received bruises in the wrestling ring that prove it.

Swish. Kyoko tosses the rope across. It falls through the air and misses us completely. She tries again. *Swish. Slap.*

Holding the candle high, Yoshi tries to help her see. Taji has a better idea.

"Close your eyes," he calls.

I hold my breath as she stands blind at the edge of the drop.

"Imagine you are roping Uma," Taji yells. "See how he runs from you. Past Mikko. Past Niya. Quick, he's getting away. Throw! Throw now!"

Without thinking, Kyoko flings the rope.

"Got it." Taji raises his hand just in time to stop the end from smacking him in the nose.

"Sorry." Kyoko giggles. She doesn't *look* sorry.

The goldfish in my stomach sprout wings and flap

against my insides as Nezume ties the rope around his waist. What if he slips and the rope doesn't hold? But Nezume's not worried. He scurries across the ledge and throws the rope back.

With one arm and a sprained ankle, it won't be easy for Mikko. Suddenly the harness rope doesn't seem safe at all.

Mikko shuffles slowly, but he isn't afraid. Halfway across, he leans back against the wall and waves. "Look, no hands!"

Everyone laughs. It's not easy for him, but he's making it look easy to help us. And it's working. My goldfish are quiet now.

Taji follows next. Then it's my turn. I shouldn't look down, but I can't help it. Even in the pale and reflected candlelight, I can see it's a long drop. The White Crane flaps its sodden wings in panic. I knot the rope in place, take a deep breath, and think about my friends on the other side. Braver now, I step onto the narrow ledge and edge my way toward them.

A crowd of hands reaches out for me as I scramble to safety. Now it's Yoshi's turn. For once, we get to help him. When Yoshi douses the candle, I can't see him

Taji follows next.

anymore, but I feel the rope move. When I eventually grasp his hand to help him up, my fingers touch something warm and sticky.

"Blood brothers," he whispers, reminding me of another night on a different mountain. He shakes his head because he doesn't want me to tell the others. Yoshi's more concerned about us. Especially Nezume, who looks tired and pale. Our leader understands what it's like to walk with a heavy weight on your shoulders.

"It's my turn to help Mikko now," Yoshi says.

Nezume shakes his head. "Thanks, but I can manage." It's a matter of honor, and Nezume will faint on his feet before he gives in. He helped to cut off Mikko's arm, but now, for the length of this journey, he has the chance to replace it.

Still, Yoshi can see Nezume needs to rest. "I think we should stop for dinner."

I agree. My stomach is growling louder than Yoshi's Tiger, and says it's long past dinnertime. If things were different, it would be fun to sit in the gloom with my friends. But our rice cakes are soggy and the dried fish is waterlogged. It's so cold. I just want to escape from the tunnel.

We eat quickly, without talking, until Yoshi moves us on.

"Time to go," he says, handing the candle to Kyoko to relight.

The slow tramp begins again. *Squish. Squelch.* Sandals slap and slosh. One saturated footstep after another.

"Did you hear that?" Taji whispers.

We shake our heads, but we know something is happening. Taji always hears things first. Nezume's nose twitches. He can feel it.

Now I can hear and feel it, too. A low rumble and the ground trembles. There's more mud coming.

"I know a different way out." Nezume points to a hole in the wall ahead. "See? We can take the higher path. It's longer, but it's above the mud flow. I've never been that way, but I'm sure it leads outside. I can smell it."

We trust Nezume's rat-like nose as much as Taji's bat ears. Yoshi waves us forward. One by one, we climb onto his shoulders, to be hoisted into the gap. Nezume scrambles through first. Struggling together, we drag our leader up last.

The new tunnel is warmer, with the promise of an end in sight. The passage immediately widens into a small cave. I can hop and twirl and swing my arms without bruising my knuckles. My friends copy my dance until, like a tangle of kite strings, we collapse in a heap together.

But we're not the only ones there. A skeleton sits cross-legged in the middle of the cave.

Sensei says a samurai should be able to look death in the eye. I fix my stare on empty eye sockets and bow low. We all do. At first, no one says anything. It's easy to respect the dead, but it's hard to include them in conversation.

"Gaiya," I finally mumble, bringing the ghost story to life.

Now we know what happened to him. In traditional times, when a samurai wanted to atone for dishonor, he committed *seppuku*, taking his sword and slicing open his belly. Only Gaiya's bones remain, but his sword protrudes from where his stomach once was.

Kyoko eyes the skeleton with dismay. "I thought Sensei said Gaiya found peace."

"He did," Nezume says. "He found a way to restore his honor." Nezume understands best of all. With Mikko needing help, Rat Boy's honor is also returned. The heavier Mikko leans, the higher Nezume's spirit soars.

"But Gaiya was a good sensei. Ki-Yaga said so. How could such a wise man fall from grace?" Taji wonders.

Yoshi sits down. He's ready to share his burden. "I want to tell you why I won't fight," he says. "Sometimes dishonor falls like lightning. It strikes whoever stands in the wrong place at the wrong time."

We form a tight circle around Yoshi. We're lucky. We're all in the right place, whatever the time, as long as we're with one another. If Gaiya had walked with friends, I'm sure he would have made it through the mountain, too.

"I told Niya this story when we went down to the village together," Yoshi starts softly. "Now I'm ready to tell it again."

I listen as he repeats the tale of the boy who rolled down the cliff side. The one who, unlike me, he couldn't bring back. Gaiya isn't the only one to find peace in the mountain. Nezume walks with a light heart, and now Yoshi has left his troubles here in the tunnel.

Kyoko hugs him tight. The rest of us don't need to. She hugs hard enough for all of us, and Yoshi knows how we feel.

"We need to get going. The light won't last much longer." Mikko points at the candle, now nothing but a dirty puddle of wax.

"We're almost at the end," Nezume says.

Before I have a chance to breathe a sigh of relief, the candle splutters and fades. The last glow of light is just enough to illuminate the grin on Taji's face. I don't know what he's got to be pleased about. What if there's another deep hole right in front of the tunnel mouth? Then Gaiya won't be alone anymore. He'll have our bones to keep him company.

"I don't need to see to find my way out," Taji says. "Follow me."

As he leads us forward, the soft sound of wings fills

the cavern. There's nothing ghostly about it. I can feel the warmth of Gaiya's smile on my back. The Golden Bat leads us through the darkness, toward the stars and the tunnel's end.

"We made it." Nezume's voice ricochets across the moonlit mountains.

It's a short drop to the ground and we're safe. Even the taunts and teasing of the Games can't take this victory away from me.

"*Chi!*" Taji yells, grabbing a vine and swinging down to the ground.

"*Jin!*" Yoshi pulls Kyoko and me with him.

"*Yu!*" Mikko bellows as he and Nezume jump together.

We're muddy, wet, and smelly. It's a badge of honor, not bright and shiny like a medal, but we wear it like a uniform. One look at us and you can see we're a team.

Chi, jin, yu.

Wisdom, benevolence, and courage.

And something even more powerful than a samurai sword.

Friendship.

CHAPTER ELEVEN

忠
誠

TSURUGIDĀKE
TEMPLE

"Wake up, lazybones. It's lunchtime."

Yoshi pulls my pack from underneath my head. Dragging my blurry eyes open, I squint into the sun, already high overhead. My stomach immediately complains about missed breakfast.

"Thanks to Nezume's directions and strong shoulders, we have made good progress," says Yoshi. "We'll still be at the Games on time."

Rat Boy beams. Mud brown, he's a Cockroach now.

"I know another shortcut," he announces. Nezume knows the mountain inside out.

We eat lunch fast. If there was a speed-eating event at the Games, we would be sure to win. Mikko is the first to finish. He rises slowly and leans his weight on his injured ankle, a smile spreading across his face.

"I'm two-legged again!" he shouts.

"Good, because we need Nezume to go first." Yoshi

motions Rat Boy to the front of our line. No longer a stranger, he is our friend and guide.

"You never know where you will find a friend," Sensei told us. "Once I found one under my bed."

That's where Sensei discovered the samurai who gave him Uma. The samurai was hiding from three men who wanted to kill him. Our master never told us why.

"You do not need to know everything. Sometimes it is better not to know."

I looked under my bed every day for a month, but I never found anyone.

"What do you expect to find?" asked Mikko. "Ants for friends?"

"None of your business," I said. "You do not need to know everything."

Half an hour later, the temple appears beneath the late afternoon mist. The jewel of Mount Tsurugidake is made of polished white stone. Six gleaming turrets stretch skyward. Directly behind the temple are the tournament rings for wrestling and sword fighting, the river for swimming, and fields where the horses graze.

On the main steps, the four eldest Komusu wait to

greet the arriving teams. One hundred priests live and serve at the temple, but only these four are allowed to speak. After the Games are over, they won't talk again for another year.

Number One, the Master of the Games, stands in front of Number Two, Number Three, and Number Four. The Komusu don't waste words on names. The Games Master's curly white beard reaches to the hem of his long pink robe. The other three wear yellow, orange, and red, to symbolize the rising and setting of the sun.

The world is a strange place when the wisest and holiest of priests is an old man in a pink dress. Wisdom must be color-blind, with no fashion sense.

The priests bob and nod their heads in welcome. They say NOTHING. It's the Zen thing, but it's probably easier just to nod when you wear a basket from head to shoulder.

"The Komusu are wise beyond speech," Sensei told us. "It is a privilege to hear their words. You must show great respect."

The Master of the Games opens his mouth. We bow low, scraping the ground with appreciation for what he is about to say. What difference can a little more dirt make to our dirty faces? Sometimes it's easy to be respectful.

"Welcome. I see Ki-Yaga teaches his students well. Your master is waiting for you in the eastern wing."

Number Three leads us through the temple entrance, into the large foyer where the indoor events take place. He points to the eastern wing, bows, and leaves. Pausing, we admire the huge golden gong, which will call us together for the Opening Ceremony.

Other teams are already wandering around. They stare, whispering about our odd appearance. We looked strange before, but now we're covered in mud and smell like swamp monsters. Kyoko has leaves in her hair, and my ears are caked with slime.

Squish. Squelch. Our sandals drip as we walk.

"The frog made it out of the pond," someone sneers, pointing at me.

"Looks like he brought the pond with him," another says, and snickers.

"Hey, freak girl's hair is almost the right color."

"There's a mole man."

Everywhere kids hoot with laughter.

"They've got a drowned rat with them," says a Dragon Boy, recognizing Nezume.

Nezume winks. "What's that smell? I think I smell smoke. Maybe a Dragon belch."

"Bur-urp," Kyoko says loudly. There's nothing ladylike about Kyoko.

"No, it's worse than that. Must be a Dragon fart," I say, remembering Onaku's joke about the Dragon Master.

We can't hear their taunts anymore. Our laughter is too loud.

When we reach our quarters, Sensei is waiting. Seven beds form a ring around the room. Sensei knew we'd bring Rat Boy. A bronze kimono lies folded on the extra pillow. Mr. and Mrs. Onaku knew, too.

Sensei studies our filthy faces.

"Very good. I see you did extra wrestling practice on the way. In an hour we gather for the Opening Ceremony, so you need to bathe. Niya, you are the muddiest. You can go first."

"Yes, Sensei." I gather up my towel and head down the corridor to the bathroom.

"Off for a swim, little frog?" says a passing Snake boy with a giggle.

Saying nothing, I clutch my towel against my chest. Teams are not allowed to fight except in Games events. If it were up to me, I'd swing my crutch and smack him around the ears. Sensei is right. A true samurai doesn't need a sword. A bamboo crutch will do fine.

The bath is filled with cool, mountain spring water. I sink until, like a frog, only my eyes are visible. Fear of failure floats away with the mud. There is nothing wrong with being a frog. Maybe, when I am Sensei, I will build the Frog Ryu.

"Maybe you will," the wizard says inside my head. "But now it is time to hop out and let someone else bathe."

When I return to the room, Mikko heads off to the bath. I hear the jeers follow him down the hallway. Mikko's voice echoes back to me, "If I draw you in the sword-fighting match, I will chop off both your arms. Then it will be my turn to laugh when the wolf drags his snout in the dirt."

Sensei is listening, too.

"Insults make us strong. They bind us together and separate us from the false samurai, the ones who do not follow Bushido. Many men have called me names," Sensei pauses to smile, "but they are without voices now."

Only a fool would insult Sensei's honor. Soon we are clean and wrapped in towels. Sensei looks at the sun. "Time to dress."

Shaking the traveling creases from my new kimono, I watch Sensei unroll his pack. Mrs. Onaku has made him a kimono, too. A ragtag line of brown cockroaches runs across the sash. Some cockroaches have missing legs and arms. One is much bigger than the others. The one in the middle has no eyes. Another has a white head, and on the end is a little one, with a long tail.

Unstringing another package, Sensei reveals our *hachimaki,* traditional headbands. Symbols of honor and determination, they are embroidered with the same cockroaches that scurry across Sensei's sash.

The headbands bind our foreheads and tie us together. Cockroach Ryu is a team. Things that make us different are no longer important. When we put our uniforms on, we're ready to battle a whole world of Dragons.

"It's not the individual parts that matter," Sensei says. "It is what you create when you join the pieces." He drapes his tattered brown cloak over his shining kimono, and the old and the new merge together before my eyes.

Only Nezume is not ready.

"Don't you like your uniform?" Kyoko asks.

"I like it very much, but I'm not competing."

"You're still an important part of our team," says Mikko. "You're our cheerleader, and we desperately need one of those."

"But I am not even a warrior student." Hanging his head, Nezume stares at the ground.

"Close your eyes and kneel," instructs Sensei.

He takes a razor from his pack and shaves two samurai stripes in Nezume's hair. Then he twists the rat tail up into a topknot. Raising Nezume's sword, he taps him on one shoulder.

"Rise, Nezume, warrior student of the Cockroach Ryu. Every samurai must come when he is called, and

I am calling you now. Gembuku is not bound by time or place."

On his feet again, Nezume opens his eyes and smiles. He drops his old kimono to the ground, revealing his back, criss-crossed with deep scars.

Sensei's face darkens like thunder.

"Who did this?" he demands, but I can tell he already knows.

"The Dragon Master," Nezume whispers.

"Why?" Sensei's eyes flash like lightning. A terrible storm is gathering.

"I was ashamed of what happened to Mikko. I refused to say it was right. When three fight against one, there is no victory in winning. Only dishonor. The Dragon Master did not agree. He taught my lesson with a bamboo cane, but I did not listen."

The White Crane wraps a protective wing around the Long-Tailed Rat. Nezume is safe now.

"You are a much greater and wiser samurai than your old master ever will be," says Sensei. "Put on your new kimono, and wear it with great pride. Your Dragon days are over. I am your master now, Little Cockroach."

Bong. Bong-ong-ong.

The gong sounds to call the *ryu* teams to the ceremony. I count seven teams in a sea of bright uniforms and headbands. It's a good number.

"I feel lucky," says Kyoko, showing me all six fingers crossed.

Number One speaks in a soft voice, furry from lack of speech.

"Boar Ryu," he announces. *Bong.* The gong sounds a welcome note.

The students of the Boar line up in the front row, their master at the head of the line. They spread their muscled legs in a fighting stance and crouch down low. Boar samurai are famous for their strength and stamina.

"Uh-uh. Yah!" Bowing low to the Komusu elders, they pound out the traditional samurai battle cry.

Behind me, someone from the Dragon Ryu grunts and snuffles like a pig. They wouldn't do that if they had ever been chased by a boar. Even a Dragon wouldn't be brave facing Black Tusk. I lick my lips in memory.

Chance places us before the Dragons, but that won't

last long. They'll soon be in front of us all, in the place where only winners stand.

"Cockroach Ryu." Another strike of the gong.

We line up in the second row. Our bronze kimonos shine like gold in the afternoon sunlight flowing through the windows. It's not easy to crouch on one leg, but Yoshi holds me steady. Sensei thumps his staff on the ground.

"Uh-uh. Yah!" We yell and punch the air with both hands. Except Mikko, of course, but he strikes twice as hard with his one fist. Our cry rings out loud and proud. Yoshi's deep voice booms through the temple.

"Dragon Ryu." The gong pounds.

Awed silence stalks the room. Compared to their red and gold kimonos blazing like fire, our bronze uniforms look brown again. The Dragon Master holds out his arm, and the line crouches. "Uh-uh. Yah! Yah-ahh!" Low and menacing. Victorious before the Games even begin.

We might as well go home. It's already over. Beside me, Yoshi doesn't agree. The Tiger growls to accept the challenge.

Our bronze kimonos shine like gold.

Roll call continues. "Eagle Ryu."

The Eagles kick high. A soft whistle escapes from Mikko.

"Rabbit Ryu." "Snake Ryu." "Wolf Ryu."

As each *ryu* team is introduced, the gong sounds. Each line assumes their position and shouts their battle cry. Finally all seven teams are in place. It's time for the Opening Ceremonial Dance.

The drum beats. Punching the air, we kick high. I land on my foot every time, and I'm glad of the hours spent practicing. Then I hear a whispered snicker as my leg is kicked out from under me. I fall flat on my face. No one dares to laugh in front of the Komusu, but I can feel the mockery rippling through the room.

The White Crane hides its head beneath a wing. It's worse than last year already, and my one leg wants to run home. My face is bright red as Sensei helps me to my feet.

The Komusu stand too. They expect an explanation.

"The boy tripped," the Dragon Master says. "I saw

it. I am standing right behind him. If he can't stand up properly, he shouldn't be here."

The Komusu don't nod. They wait for me to speak. How can I argue with the Dragon Master? Insults make us strong. A true samurai doesn't need a sword. Follow Bushido. Sensei's teachings come to my rescue. I feel sorry for the Dragon Master, who has forgotten what it means to be a samurai.

"*Chi. Jin. Yu.*" I bow my head.

The Komusu nod so hard I worry their baskets will fall off.

"Excellent," Sensei whispers in my ear. "You have made a big impression. A loud thump followed by wise words. No one could miss that."

The gong sounds again. The ceremony — and my humiliation — are over. We are free to wander the temple until the Games begin tomorrow morning.

"How do the Komusu judge what they can't see?" Mikko asks.

"They know," I answer. "When one is truly wise, he knows."

Like Sensei. He knows everything.

"Let's go for a walk in the gardens," Sensei suggests. "Perhaps I can find a tree to sit and meditate under."

He doesn't fool us. Our master wants to sleep and dream.

Flowers grow everywhere. Cherry blossoms on the trees, lotus blossoms on the pond. While the others admire and sniff the blooms, I study the crow-claw imprints Sensei's knobbly toes leave in the rain-soaked soil. Kyoko's words echo inside my head. Sensei can't be a *tengu*. He doesn't make mistakes. He's perfect.

"Have you ever made a mistake, Sensei?" I ask.

He looks at me with eyes that care. Sad eyes.

"Everyone makes mistakes, little Niya. It's how we become wise."

Sensei's wisdom is infinite. He must have made a very big mistake.

CHAPTER TWELVE

THE SAMURAI GAMES: DAY ONE

Sword fighting is the first event of the day. My opponent is a small, thin boy from the Eagle Ryu. He got lucky. He probably couldn't beat anyone except me.

Yesterday's rain has disappeared, and the early morning sun warms my back. No cloud would dare interrupt the Games. The Komusu priests would never allow it.

A big group has gathered in the temple grounds—Sensei and my friends, all the Eagle kids, some Dragons and Snakes, and a lone Wolf. They've all come to watch me. I'm the only one-legged samurai kid in Japan, famous for falling face-first in the dirt.

With arm raised, Number One stands beside the big circular gong where the names of past winners are inscribed. The dragon's tail winds around so many times that I lose count. Not a single cockroach scuttles across the gold. We're not winners, and my first match isn't going to change that.

My opponent and I face each other, a sword length apart. I bow low — slowly and carefully, so I don't tip over. The Eagle boy bows low too. When he straightens, I search his eyes for laughter. But the Eagle boy smiles at me, a big friendly grin.

Number One lets his arm fall. *Dong-g-g.* The gong echoes across the mountains.

"*Chi,*" I yell.

"*Jin.*" My opponent answers the challenge.

"*Yu.*" I check his sword thrust with a hard clash above our heads. I'm taller than him, so for a few seconds I have the advantage.

"Yay, Niya!" Nezume cheers from the sideline.

But my one leg eventually brings me down, with a hard crash into the dirt. My moment of glory is over. I can't match the Eagle boy's flying twists and kicks.

Beside me I hear someone croak, softly at first, then loud enough for everyone to hear. Laughter echoes through the crowd.

"Ignore them," says the Eagle boy, helping me to my feet. He points to my nose. "Are you hurt?"

I shake my head. "It's an old injury. I am the White Crane," I say. "I am not a frog."

"I know." He bows low. "I am the Small Shrike. It was a great honor to battle with one of Ki-Yaga's pupils."

"Thank you. The Eagle Ryu's acrobatics are beyond comparison. It was a privilege to see such skill," I respond.

Samurai study how to be polite. It's part of the Bushido code.

"It is important to show good manners," Sensei teaches. "You should always say please and thank you when chopping off an opponent's body parts."

My newfound friend and I turn and bow to the Komusu judges, who award a point to the Eagle Ryu.

"Did you see that?" I say when I join the others. "He didn't laugh at me."

"Those Eagle kids are okay," agrees Yoshi. "They weren't making rude noises."

"You were great," Kyoko adds.

190

Taji slaps me on the back, and Mikko punches me in the arm.

"Thanks," I say, but in my heart the White Crane wishes it had won.

"You are a winner," the wizard Ki-Yaga says, reading my mind. "It is much harder to win an opponent's friendship than to score a point at sword fighting."

"My turn next," says Mikko. "I don't think I'll be making any friends." He slashes his sword through the air. "I've got a Wolf to skin."

Because he only has one arm, Mikko has a big advantage. The Wolf boy thinks he's going to win easily, but before he can thrust forward, Mikko has already pierced his leather chest plate. It's all over.

"No-o-o-o!" the Wolf boy howls in frustration.

Mikko's win scores our first point, but it doesn't last long. Yoshi refuses to fight and forfeits his match, so a penalty is deducted. By the end of the sword fighting events, we've struggled our way up to zero.

The wrestling events are next. Kyoko is matched against an enormous Dragon boy. All the Dragons have come to laugh at the freak girl.

"Hey, white monkey monster, where's that extra finger?" they call.

Kyoko lets them know. She sticks it in the air with a rude gesture. If you ask me, the Dragon boy is the strange-looking one. He is square like a piece of sushi, with beady, black eyes, and a nasty smile. He smells fishy, as if someone left him out in the sun.

Admiring glances follow the Dragon Master as he struts around the wrestling ring, his red silk cape billowing behind him. No one pays attention to Sensei waiting patiently. When he notices Nezume standing with us, the Dragon Master stops and glares.

"What's he doing here?" the Dragon Master thunders. "He belongs to the Dragon Ryu." The thunder drops to a low rumble. "Come and stand with me, boy."

Shaking his head, Nezume hides behind Sensei.

"Three years ago the boy was a Dragon. But now, he belongs to the Cockroach Ryu." Sensei's tone is cold and threatening, like a sword hanging over the Dragon Master's head. No one says anything. No one moves. We hold our breath and wait to see if the sword drops.

When the Dragon Master laughs, we all breathe

again. "You always did pick up what everyone else threw away, Ki-Yaga. If you want him, he's yours. He has the heart of a cockroach anyway."

I put my arm around Nezume, to show my support and to make sure I don't fall over in anger.

Sensei bows politely to the Dragon Master. "The heart of a cockroach beats even after its head has been cut off, but the poor dragon has no heart at all. Your compliment is accepted."

Before the Dragon Master can reply, the gong booms. *Boom, boom.* The Dragon Master's retort will have to wait.

Kyoko's not afraid of her big opponent. Her Snow Monkey spirit knows every wrestling trick. The two lock arms and drop to the ground. Kyoko presses the Dragon boy's face into the dust. Spluttering, he whispers something into her ear. Pink eyes blaze with anger.

"What did he say?" I ask Taji. A whisper is like a yell in Taji's ear. I know. I once whispered to Yoshi where I hid a bowl of honey pudding. When I went to get it, Taji had eaten it.

"The Dragon boy said, 'If you think an extra finger helps, try wrestling with none.'"

"What does that mean?" Mikko asks.

The Dragon boy answers Mikko's question. Rolling his shoulder onto Kyoko's hand, he grinds it into the ground. Kyoko turns as white as her hair, and pain streaks her face. The Komusu judges rise to their feet, basket heads bobbing fast. Number Two bangs the gong to signal that a penalty will be deducted if it happens again. But the damage is done. Cradling her hand in pain, Kyoko is unable to continue. The Dragon boy stands over her, ready to claim his victory.

Beside me, the Tiger roars. Yoshi leaps to his feet.

"Let me wrestle!" he shouts.

The Dragon boy shakes his head. "You can't. It's against the rules," he sneers.

"What rule is above Bushido?" Sensei asks the Komusu. "What is more important than honor, courage, and duty to a friend?"

"A samurai must fight his own battles," the Dragon Master insists.

Sensei bows his head. "Sometimes one battle begins halfway through another. I understand that the Dragon Master is afraid of the wrestling skills of the mighty

Cockroach and is worried his student will lose. Perhaps he worries the Cockroaches will laugh at him."

The Dragon Master's eyes simmer. "Dragons are not afraid of bugs. My student will fight the Cockroach. Your boy is big, but he has no skill. I hear he is afraid of fighting and doesn't even practice. Let him make a fool of himself for this ugly girl."

Yoshi leaps into the ring. When the gong sounds, the two boys rush at each other. The Dragon boy is big, but Yoshi is strong with rage. He doesn't bother to wrestle. He picks up his opponent and tosses him out of the ring. *Ka-thump.* The Dragon boy lands at the feet of his master.

"Sometimes skill is not necessary," Sensei says loudly as he guides us away from the wrestling arena. "Let us attend to Kyoko's hand." Sensei does not look back, but I do. The Dragon Master is breathing fire.

"You're not ugly," I whisper to Kyoko. "You're the most beautiful girl here."

She looks sad. "I'm the only girl here."

"A samurai girl is rare and beautiful," Sensei says. "Even with six fingers and a swollen hand."

He picks up his opponent and tosses
him out of the ring.

Kyoko's smile outshines the sun.

The Komusu award a point to Yoshi but don't penalize Kyoko for not completing the match. Mikko loses, but Taji wins his wrestling bout. We've got two points! The most points we've ever had! I'm so excited, I can hardly eat my lunch.

Sensei has no problem scoffing three bowls of rice and egg. For a skinny old man, he eats a lot. His stick-thin arms and legs are hollow like bamboo.

"How do the Komusu see?" I ask. "They have huge thick baskets covering their heads, but they never bump into anything. Without eyes, they knew the Dragon boy cheated. Is it magic?"

"I don't believe in magic," says Yoshi. "I believe in things I can see and hear."

I believe. Especially after this morning. Scoring two points at the Games is magic to my eyes and ears.

Sensei puts his chopsticks down. A lesson is coming. Nothing else would stop him mid-meal. "Anything that is not understood is magic. Are there things you do not understand, Yoshi?"

"Yes, Sensei. There are many things."

"Then there is much magic. If you cannot see or hear something, that does not mean it is not there."

It's true. I fall over things in the dark all the time. I never see them, but they're always there.

"If only the things I can see exist, then it's a pretty empty world!" adds Taji. "The Komusu are like me. They see with their ears."

Our teacher nods. The lesson has been learned, and Sensei returns to his bowl.

Number One pounds the gong to signal the end of lunch. I groan so loud, I'm sure Number Three looks right at me through his basket. It's poetry time. The next event is haiku.

The topic is something I know a lot about— NOTHING. Even that can't rescue me. I'd rather fall on my face in the sword-fighting ring than write a poem. But Sensei says haiku is important.

"A samurai must be able to write his own epitaph in the middle of battle. In case of sudden death. It is not worth dying if no one knows about it."

It doesn't matter to me. Writing the poem is more likely to kill me than any sword thrust. I'll die of boredom.

I quickly scrawl some words on the page to make sure I don't get a point deducted. Then I help Kyoko. She's our best poet, but her swollen hand can't hold the brush.

"You tell me what to write," I say.

Taji is struggling, too. It's hard to know where to start when you can't see the page. He puts his brush down. Even though he's written nothing, he's smiling like the bat that swallowed the beetle.

Dong-g-g. Time is up. We all put our brushes down. Number Two walks around the room, reading the poems through his basket. When he reaches Taji, he gasps out loud. Poor kid. Now everyone will laugh. It's not his fault he can't see the page. He did his best.

Number Two calls over Number One, and Three and Four. They all gasp. It's a rare moment, when four Komusu priests open their mouths at the same time.

"Perfect," Number One says. "This is the greatest poem ever written at a Games."

I sneak a look. Maybe Taji wrote something after all. No. His poem is an empty page.

The Dragon Master is not impressed. One of his

students is Taji's opponent. Even though the Dragons are not skilled poets, they expected to beat a blind kid.

"That's not a poem," the Dragon Master protests. "Where is the required format? The first line must have five syllables, the second seven, and the third five. How can a poem with none of these win?"

The Komusu crowd around Taji's page. They nod to each other excitedly. Even more than usual.

"The judges' decision is unanimous. It is beyond question," announces Number One. "The poem is found to have the correct lines and syllables, each containing NOTHING. The poem is without flaw. We have decided to award the Cockroach Ryu an additional point for extreme excellence."

It's probably the longest speech a Komusu ever made. No one dares argue with that.

My poem doesn't score a point, but I helped Kyoko win. We're up to five points! We've won a point in every event so far. The last event before dinner is *ikebana,* flower arranging. I'm the only hope we've got. Kyoko's injured hand can't hold a flower, and I'm not allowed to place them for her. Mikko's arrangements always turn out lopsided. Yoshi's look like he just jams them in—which he does. Taji is good with shape, but he can't hear colors.

On the *ikebana* table are three cherry blossom sprays, a lotus flower, and some greenery, representing earth, sky, and nature. A world of beauty. I close my eyes and breathe deeply. *Om. Om. Om.*

"To arrange flowers, you must first find beauty within yourself," Sensei teaches. "And if you cannot find it there, look around you."

The White Crane can see for miles.

There are two beautiful things in my life. Mrs. Onaku is a cherry blossom woman, and Kyoko is a lotus flower girl. Perfectly balanced, neither is more beautiful than the other. I place the woman and child between the green of heaven and earth and step back to survey my opponent's effort. A Bear boy is a follower of Yoshi's "shove them in" approach. Samurai warriors are champion *ikebana* artists, but samurai kids don't like flower arranging at all.

The judges admire my work. I know because they nod a lot.

Sensei translates the nodding. "The judges see sky mother and earth child. They see great beauty." He grins. "But all I can see are Mrs. Onaku and Kyoko." The wizard sees everything.

On the board at the temple entrance, the scores are posted. The Dragons are in the lead, but we have six points. Yah-yah! We're not coming last.

At dinner, the Eagle boy finds me. He's brought a friend with him.

"Can we join you?" he says. "This is Inu. He's our haiku specialist. He wants to meet Taji." Inu sits next to Taji, and they are soon chattering like a pair of bats. Taji likes Inu. I know because he's telling him his favorite joke.

"'I see', said the blind man, who didn't see at all." A good joke lets you laugh at yourself and it doesn't hurt when other people do, too. Inu's warm laughter is contagious, and catches us all.

The Dragons are listening, but they don't think Taji's joke is funny.

"You should know, Mole Man," jeers the big kid Yoshi wrestled.

Beside me, Nezume gnashes his teeth and Mikko's glare cuts like his sword.

Yoshi rises to stand in front of the big kid, ready to defend his team's honor. "Pick on someone your own size," he says.

From nowhere, Sensei appears beside Yoshi. Not even Taji heard him approach.

"Is there a problem?" he asks.

"None of your business, old man," the Dragon boy sneers.

"My students are my business. I am not like your master." Sensei places his fingers on the Dragon boy's neck. I know that feeling. It's scary when you can't move a muscle. The Dragon boy's eyes are bulging, and his face is fright white.

Sensei removes his hand and waves his staff in the air. "Be gone. Quickly, before I turn you into stone."

Intrigued, the White Crane turns its beady eye to watch. Can he really do that? I wonder.

The Dragons don't wait to find out.

CHAPTER THIRTEEN

THE SAMURAI GAMES: DAY TWO

After breakfast the next morning, we head for the archery area. It's my turn first. Maybe I'll win. Before, I couldn't complete the riding session of the archery event because Uma wasn't interested in victory. All he wanted to do was throw me off and join in the laughter. But Uma is on our team now that my pockets are full of honey pudding.

Sensei leads Uma over. Our horse sniffs my jacket and smiles.

My opponent is a Dragon on a sleek black steed. Uma snorts rudely at them. In his hand, the Dragon boy holds a bow carved from expensive wood. His arrows are silver tipped, with bright feathers tied to the ends. I made my own bow, carving it carefully from one of Sensei's cherry trees. The wooden stave is slightly crooked, but strung with arrow in place, it sings like a sword.

"It is right for a bow to be made of cherry wood.

As the cherry is among flowers, the samurai is among men," Sensei says.

It's an old traditional saying. The life of a samurai is one of sacrifice, sometimes as short as the three days of the cherry blossom.

Th-twang. I test the string on my bow. I don't intend to sacrifice anything on the archery field—not points, not pride. Looking at the White Crane feather on the end of each shaft, I know my arrows will fly true.

Double points are scored every time an arrow hits a moving target. Waving to my friends, I climb onto Uma's back. He races like a horse possessed. Uma has always been crazy, but today he runs with the bloodlust of battle in his flaring nostrils. He wants to win. When the targets are counted, Uma and I have six and the Dragon boy has two. Holding his head high, Uma sneezes in the Dragon boy's direction.

"Yuck," the boy yells as thick globs of mucus land on his head and his horse. The Dragon horse grunts at Uma. Samurai are very polite, but their horses are not.

Sensei is quick to apologize and offers his dirty white handkerchief.

Uma has always been crazy, but today he runs
with the bloodlust of battle in his flaring nostrils.

Doubly disgusted, the boy backs away.

"You did that on purpose, you old wizard," the Dragon Master accuses.

The Dragon boy spits at Sensei's feet.

Sensei shakes his head.

"I am not a magician. I do not control horses. And you are not a teacher if you cannot control your students," he says, turning his back on the fuming Dragon.

Still targets are next. I shoot a perfect score, and the Dragon boy misses when Sensei blows his nose. I've won!

My friends crowd around to congratulate me, offering Uma palms smeared with honey pudding. Uma likes Kyoko's hands best. They're soft, and you can fit more honey pudding on six fingers.

"Well done." Yoshi slaps me on the back. "You won a point and defended Sensei's honor. Maybe with Uma's help, we'll all win a point at archery."

"It was as if Uma had wings," Nezume says.

Uma does, with the White Crane perched on his back.

When I reach the calligraphy room, my confidence drops to the bottom of Mount Tsurugidake. First we have to write the *kanji* symbol for a word from the Bushido code. Even though we practice the words with Sensei every day, I still make a mess.

I'm glad the days of war are over, but some samurai peacetime skills are deadly boring. Almost as dangerous as being in a real battle. When I am Sensei of the Frog Ryu, I will invent a new practice. Instead of the Komusu's wisdom without words, I will teach wisdom without writing.

"But what about the students who cannot hear?" the wizard asks inside my head.

"I will show them," the future Sensei of the Frog Ryu answers.

"Aaaah," my teacher sighs, pleased.

Today's word is *chi,* wisdom. There's more ink on my hands than on the page, but the black smudge is enough to ensure that I don't lose a point. Sitting next to me, a Snake boy knows how to wield a brush. The ink on his page runs like water into wisdom.

He notices me staring at his work. "You're not allowed to copy," he hisses, hiding the *kanji* with his hands.

"I'm not. I've finished. I was admiring your lettering.

Mine looks like bird feet." The White Crane looks guilty as I show the Snake boy my page. He smiles at the blotches.

Number Two announces the second task, a string of *kanji* that forms a saying. Now my memory gives me an advantage and compensates for my sloppy brushwork. There are over 800,000 *kanji,* and I have crammed more in my brain than any other samurai kid. I'll do better this time.

"The past must be visited to learn the future," Number Three reads.

A brushstroke of luck! All the Cockroaches know that one. It's one of Sensei's favorites. Sensei trains us in the traditional ways, but he also teaches that a samurai must be able to take the old ways and adjust them to the new. But not with flashy red silk coats, cheating tricks, and lack of honor — not like the Dragons. He means by applying Bushido. *Chi, jin, yu.* Wisdom, benevolence, and courage. Like we did with Nezume. Like I did at the Opening Ceremony.

The Snake Boy positions his hand so I can see his work. He trusts me now.

"I hope you win," I whisper.

When the *kanji* phrases are judged, the Snake boy gets an extra point for excellence.

"Well done." I bow low. "I would have awarded two extra points."

"Thank you." The Snake boy bows lower. I've made another friend.

We all score a point except Taji—who knows the *kanji* but can't see the page to write them on. "Did you see the updated point scores?" he asks.

"No. And neither did you," I say. We both laugh.

"I don't need to. I added them up in my head. You're not the only brain around here. We're doing okay."

"We're not coming last?" asks Kyoko.

"We're in the middle," announces Nezume.

The middle is good. It's safe. I like the middle way.

Sensei told us about Buddha, who taught the middle way—Right Understanding, Right Thought, Right Speech, Right Action, Right Livelihood, Right Effort, Right Mindfulness, and Right Concentration. Eight things is a lot to get right all the time.

"What is the samurai way?" I asked.

"Any path that does not result in one's head being cut off," said Sensei. "The samurai way is much simpler."

I like it that way, too.

The next event is swimming. We put on our armor and our battle helmets. It's hard for Mikko. He has to use one arm to swim and swing his sword. But Mikko doesn't give up. When he sees his opponent is a Dragon boy, he's even more determined to win. Nezume straps Mikko's sword to his chest. He's determined, too.

The Striped Gecko floats on his back out to the middle of the river.

"Look! No arms!" Mikko calls as he turns to tread water.

"Poor Mikko," I say, thinking of the embarrassment to follow.

Kyoko snaps her teeth together and wriggles her hands like a snake. "Don't worry. He's okay."

Even Nezume has a knowing smile as Mikko dives underwater.

"Dragons are not good swimmers," he says. "They are too fat. Too full of themselves."

"Aaargh." The Dragon boy yelps, getting pulled

under with a gurgle. Mikko pops up before him, and the Dragon emerges, coughing and spluttering, to meet the point of Mikko's sword.

"Foul!" the Dragon yells. "He tricked me. The Cockroach cheated."

The Dragon Master agrees and storms over to the judges to protest. In blind unison, the Komusu take the rule books out from under their baskets and call Mikko over for questioning.

"What do you have to say to the Dragon's accusations?" Number Four asks.

"I let my spirit guide me, Master." Mikko bows low, and the Komusu nod approvingly. "My spirit totem is the lizard. Sometimes I am the Striped Gecko, but today I was a reptile monster, swimming in the river mouth. A samurai must watch what is above and what is below if he wishes a victory in battle."

"What foolishness is this? There are no such monsters in Japan," the Dragon Master interrupts.

"Is it being suggested a samurai's skills are limited to Japan or to the things he knows are there?" Sensei asks, eyebrows raised like pagoda rooftops.

Nodding, the Komusu award Mikko a point. For swimming! It's a miracle even Sensei could not have created.

Next, Yoshi is competing against a Rabbit boy. It's an unlucky draw. The Rabbits are smart and fast, even underwater. As soon as the gong sounds, Yoshi's opponent disappears into the river. Yoshi follows, trying to keep pace.

"I can't see a thing," complains Mikko. "They're battling underwater."

"Does it matter what we see?" asks Sensei, resting in the sun with his eyes closed.

"Of course not," answers Taji. "Makes no difference to me at all."

Yoshi and the Rabbit boy surface with a loud splash, swords clashing. Yoshi is strong, but the Rabbit is cunning.

"What was that?" The Rabbit boy points to us on the bank.

Yoshi spins around to check. A leader's first responsibility is to his team. The Rabbit dives, and Yoshi sinks, spluttering. He emerges swordless.

Bong-ong. The gong sounds to declare the Rabbit victory. Rabbit boy dives again and retrieves Yoshi's sword.

"Thank you." Yoshi tucks his sword into his sash. "Your strategy was clever. Only a Rabbit could tunnel underwater." He climbs onto the bank and bows, wet and dripping.

"I learned from your friend." The Rabbit boy bows, too.

"I see that the clever Cockroaches have invented a new technique for combat," Taji comments.

"How can you see anything without eyes?" asks Nezume, bewildered.

"You'll get used to it." I drop my voice to whisper. "Never tell secrets near Taji. He can't see, but he hears everything."

"I heard that," Taji calls.

One day he will be Komusu. He's practicing already.

The last event is origami, an individual event, where everyone can score a point. We're all skilled at paper folding, but anything can happen at the end of a long day. Our arms and legs are tired. Our hands are cramped and numb. I feel disappointed for Kyoko. She was determined to make the cockroach, but her crushed fingers can't do the complicated twists and turns.

The Dragons don't care. They crowd around, waiting to laugh when she fails. Kyoko struggles with the paper. Frustrated, she rolls it into a ball and throws it on the floor.

"Can't you make anything? I thought you had an extra finger just for this," jeers the kid who crushed her hand.

Kyoko rolls another ball and aims it at his head. The ball is packed solid and thrown hard. *Thwack!* Now I am not the only one with a flattened nose.

"She hit me," the Dragon whines.

No one pays attention. The Komusu don't notice. Or pretend not to. I make the White Crane. We all make our spirit guides; even Kyoko manages the Snow Monkey. Yoshi's Tiger crouches in front, standing guard.

The Dragon students all make the same creature: the great winged dragon. Each animal is carefully folded, and every team member scores a point.

"A strong team is made up of individuals, not poor copies," Sensei comments.

"There is no weakness in sameness. I make my students in my own image," retorts the Dragon Master.

"Poor Dragon students. Flawed to begin with." Sensei shakes his head.

The Dragon Master pretends not to hear, but wisps of smoke seem to escape his ears.

"I wish I had a different totem from them," whispers Nezume.

"You were never really a Dragon," Yoshi says. "Some spirit totems are hard to find. I found mine in the middle of an earthquake."

"Then I'll keep searching until I find my true totem."

Yoshi grins. "You already have, Rat Boy. The Long-Tailed Rat is loyal, cunning, and smart. Able to guide his friends through the maze or tunnel."

Sensei braids his beard into a thin, white rat's tail.

Despite her pain, Kyoko folds an origami rat and hands it to Nezume. His eyes shine with pride.

"If anyone can make a cockroach, it's you. Even with one hand," Nezume says.

"He's right," Mikko agrees. "Use your left hand.

It's not hard to do things one-handed. I do it all the time."

Kyoko hugs them both. Balancing her hand against the bench, she twists the paper. Slowly. Painfully. It's going to take a long time. If a river can carve a tunnel, then Kyoko can fold a cockroach.

"That's real courage," I hear a Snake boy whisper.

"Look how clever her fingers are," says a Boar boy.

Eventually the Cockroach takes its place with our spirit totems. Beside them, a skinny stick-figure man waves his staff.

"Two extra points are awarded," Number One announces. "The Cockroach student has made a perfect paper trilogy — her self, her *ryu* team, and her master."

The Dragon Master rolls his eyes, but he doesn't argue. He's lost interest in everything except the moment when the trophy rests in his hands. It won't be long now.

Dong. Dong. Dong. The gong sounds three times to end the final event. It's time for the winner to be announced. A noisy mass of samurai kids make their way to the judges' dais. The Dragons push their way through to the front. Moving aside, other schools let the winners through.

Sensei leads us to a vantage spot at the edge of the Eagles.

"I want to see this," he says.

I don't. Who wants to watch the Dragons smirk and show off? Not me.

Silence falls with a loud thud. The Komusu take their seats on the dais, then Number One rises to speak, the last words he will utter until next year.

Victory on his lips, the Dragon Master smiles broadly.

"We have a tie," Number One says. "The Dragons and the Cockroaches each have twenty-five points."

The Dragon Master glares. Other masters and their students stand open-mouthed and amazed. The Cockroaches have equaled the mighty Dragons! My crutch clatters to the floor as surprise catches me off balance. Everyone looks, but this time no one laughs. For once, they all wish they were me.

CHAPTER FOURTEEN

BATTLE OF
THE DRAGON

Fidgeting on one leg, I try to wait patiently while the Komusu judges decide our fate.

"They should let the Dragons keep the trophy. They're the current champions. No one has ever beaten them," a Wolf boy whispers.

"I want the Cockroaches to win. Those Dragons are mean and cruel. They don't deserve a trophy," murmurs an Eagle boy.

"It's embarrassing to be beaten by a bunch of bugs," says a Bear boy. Other kids mutter in agreement. No one minds losing to the great and mighty Dragons.

I'm so nervous that the goldfish in my stomach are swimming in circles, butting heads with one another. In my heart the White Crane flutters and beats its wings against my chest until it's hard to breathe.

Mumbling voices trail into silence, thick and suffocating. I want to scream out loud. Sensei looks at me as if I did, placing his fingers on his lips. I take a deep breath and the White Crane folds its wings to wait.

You cannot rush old men. The Komusu, like Sensei, stopped keeping time decades ago. Number One presses his palms together and lowers his basket-covered head. "*Om, om,*" he chants softly from beneath the tightly woven bamboo.

"*Om, om,*" the others drone in chorus.

My ear itches until I stick my finger in it and jiggle. Then my nose twitches. I can't stick my finger up there. Not with everyone watching. So I wriggle my nostrils and struggle not to sneeze. Remembering something Uma taught me, I snort backward. Like a horse. A Dragon kid elbows his friend in the ribs and points at me. I sound ridiculous. They snicker loudly, but today I don't care. I check that the Komusu are not looking, then stick out my tongue.

In front of the dais, where the Komusu sit in judgment, the Dragon Master paces backward and forward. His red silk cape billows behind him, fanning out to display a gold embroidered dragon. Fire spews from its angry mouth.

"See how magnificent his cloak is," the Wolf Master sighs in admiration.

"Yes," Sensei agrees. "There is a lot of hot air blowing out from undeneath."

His whispers echo loudly in the silence. A giggle flows through the crowd, gathering momentum until it reaches the Dragon Master. He turns and fixes Sensei with his fiery gaze. Sensei smiles and waves.

Dong-ong-ong.

A decision has been made.

"The *ryu* captains will determine a tie-breaker event," Number One announces.

Poor Yoshi. It's all up to him, and he can't even ask Sensei for help.

But Yoshi doesn't look concerned. He looks like the Cockroach that swallowed the Dragon.

"The Cockroaches will suggest the event, but the final decision will rest with the Dragons, who are the current champions," Number One continues.

The Dragon Master's face is a smug grin. He thinks it's all over, but Sensei is smiling. That means there's hope for us yet. A smile is the best disguise for an assassin. A samurai smiles when he has decided how many pieces to chop from his enemy. The Dragon Master is big and strong. It will take a lot of chopping to bring him down, but Sensei is an expert swordsman and his blade is the best Onaku ever made.

Number One motions for Yoshi to speak.

"I suggest one event, in which three selected team members will compete." Yoshi's voice booms loud and clear. It's the voice of a leader, a chopper of Dragons. "The event should be fought according to the Samurai Code so that Bushido determines the winner. The Dragons may choose the event."

My heart sinks. I can't believe my ears. Yoshi is letting the Dragons decide. They'll pick sword fighting. They've never lost a match.

The Dragon captain can't believe his ears either.

"I accept the Cockroach's suggestion. I choose sword fighting," he says.

The priests nod and bob in agreement. Number One claps his hands to seal our fate. We don't stand a chance of winning now. We're dead fish. We'll stink like *dokudami*.

But when I look at Sensei, he's grinning wider than his face. The Dragon Master is watching Sensei, too. He senses danger, but he can't see it. Neither can I. Sensei is really ancient, and the trek to the temple was difficult. Maybe he's gone crazy with old age. Maybe that's why he's smiling like a lunatic.

"Choose your competitors," Number Two instructs.

"I choose Mikko, Niya, and Taji," says Yoshi, pointing to each of us in turn.

I shake my head in disbelief. Yoshi is crazy, too.

Smirking, the Dragon captain nominates his team members. Big, strong kids with huge Cockroach-stomping feet. We haven't got a hope, so why are Sensei and Yoshi grinning like idiots? I look at Mikko, but he shrugs. I look at Kyoko, and she raises her eyebrows.

"Before we begin, there will be a reading of the Samurai Code." Number One takes his seat as Number Three rises, pulling a scroll from under his basket.

"I have no body; I make Stoicism my Body.
I have no eyes; I make the Flash of Lightning my Eyes.
I have no ears; I make Perceptiveness my Ears.
I have no limbs; I make Decisiveness my Limbs . . ."

On and on the Komusu priest drones, but I've stopped listening. No eyes. No legs. No arms.

Finally, I understand. Now a big grin spreads across my face. Who can fight best without arms, legs, and eyes? Us. We were born to fight with parts missing.

Number Three finishes reading and sits down.

"What does it mean?" the Snake Master wonders aloud.

His face like a storm cloud, the Dragon Master understands. The smiling samurai assassin knows where to place his sword, and Yoshi has placed it hard against the Dragon's throat. He's left them no room to move at all.

Number Four places a blindfold over Taji's eyes. The Dragon boy is blindfolded too. Unlike Taji, he looks confused and wary. Taji stands serene and still. In his heart the Golden Bat has woken from sleep and is listening carefully. Number Two sounds the gong. Neither boy moves, until the Dragon twitches his left foot. Taji strikes fast. Blind eyes like lightning. His sword point slices the Dragon's kimono sash.

The first tie-breaker point is ours!

Next, Number Four binds up a Dragon's leg. It's my turn in the ring. The Dragon boy hops forward, falling flat on his face at my foot. I don't laugh. I know how it feels. Instead, I offer my hand to help him up, to let him know it doesn't matter. His face red with anger and embarrassment, he shoves my arm aside. As soon as he is on his feet, he swipes recklessly at my face. It's an easy block for me. One clash and he falls over. I make an easy strike.

Another point!

The priest ties back a Dragon's arm. It's one of the boys who injured Mikko years ago, when he studied at the Dragon Ryu. Mikko points his sword straight at the boy's neck. When Sensei coughs, Mikko lowers his blade.

It's hard to swing a sword with one arm, but Mikko's weapon was specially crafted by Master Onaku. It sings as it slices across the dragon head on his opponent's vest.

The gong sounds for the final time. We've won every point!

"Yah!" Nezume yells, jumping into the air.

"Yah, yah!" I mimic. We all jump high. No one is

laughing at us now. Everyone is cheering. Everyone except the Dragons.

The Dragon Master is livid. He storms onto the dais. He takes the trophy from beside Number One and raises it high.

"This belongs to the Dragon Ryu!" he shouts. "The Cockroach Ryu cheated. They tricked us into fighting an unfair battle."

Sensei steps forward. "Was the battle any different from the one my students have always fought? Have my students cried 'Unfair!' when they fought against two arms, two legs, and two eyes? Bushido has been honored."

"I say it has not!" shouts the Dragon.

"Is the Dragon Master calling Ki-Yaga a cheat?" Sensei's voice is soft, more menacing than any bellow.

"I am." The Dragon places his hand on the hilt of his sword.

Sensei looks toward Number One. A samurai must defend his name. His sword and his name are his most valuable possessions. I wish there was another way, but the Komusu are nodding. It's too late to go back.

"Do you challenge the Cockroach Master?" Number One asks the Dragon.

"I do." The Dragon Master bows. "When I win, I will take the trophy, which never rightfully belonged to the Cockroach, and I will claim back the boy Nezume. No Dragon will study at the Cockroach Ryu ever again." He glares at Mikko.

"I accept the challenge terms." Sensei bows too, barely bending at the middle. A samurai is always polite, even when there is no respect. "Sometimes a samurai must fight, even if he does not want to," Sensei says, looking at Yoshi. Even now, Ki-Yaga is teaching.

A fight between samurai masters is a fight to the death. Sensei is a skinny old man with chopstick legs and arms. The Dragon Master is younger, and strong. It's going to be a massacre; the Dragon Master doesn't stand a chance.

At the end of the dais is a large ceremonial drum. Led by Number One, the priests begin to beat it with large sticks. An ominous rhythm.

Suddenly, the drum stops. The goldfish in my stomach flop once and die of fright.

"Choose your weapon," instructs Number One.

The Dragon Master unsheathes his *katana.* The blade glitters, cruel like the eyes of a snake. This master's sword doesn't sing; it screams for blood.

"Bring me my staff," Sensei calls. Yoshi passes the long, thick bamboo pole Sensei carries everywhere. It's not much of a weapon. He pokes it in the mud when walking and waves it in our faces when we are not listening.

"You're going to fight with that?" sneers the Dragon Master.

"A true samurai doesn't need a sword," Sensei says.

The Dragon Master laughs, and the crowd explodes in noisy guffaws.

"The Dragon will snap Ki-Yaga like that piece of old, useless bamboo," says the Wolf Master with a smirk.

Only the Eagle Master shakes his head. "Cockroaches are very hard to kill, and bamboo is very strong," he says.

Sensei smiles. He knows where to chop, even with a bamboo pole.

The drum beats again. Loud and slow. The countdown begins. Three long pounding stokes. *Boom. Boom. Boom.*

On the third boom, Sensei twirls. His long staff swings around and around. At first the Dragon Master is amused. Then frustrated. He can't touch Sensei. If he uses his sword, it will fly out of his hands. Sensei is a human hurricane.

Abruptly, he stops. We wait in the silence before the storm. The eye of the hurricane enfolds us all.

"Banzai!" Sensei whoops as he brandishes his staff.

"Ai-yah!" The Dragon Master roars as he raises his sword.

They collide with a clash of wood against steel. The ground rumbles, but there's no earthquake this time. Sensei holds his staff strong against the sword. A stalemate. The two men break apart, their eyes still locked.

The drumbeat begins again. A steady, threatening rhythm as the Dragon attempts to hypnotize its prey. Sensei sways inside the golden gaze. Then he shuts his eyes, raises one leg, and tucks his left arm behind his back. He doesn't see the Dragon smirk. He doesn't see his enemy's eyes glitter with anticipation as he moves closer.

Beside me I feel Mikko touch his sword. Kyoko's

On the the third boom, Sensei twirls.

lashes flutter, and Yoshi growls. Taji stands perfectly still, and Nezume stares with bright black eyes. The White Crane calls to its brothers and sister. Our hearts join Sensei, and together we stand against the Dragon.

Sensei moves faster than a striking snake. He wraps his raised leg around the Dragon Master, who falls hard to the ground. In triumph, Sensei raises his bamboo staff, poised to crush his opponent's skull.

The drum is silent, the crowd hushed. Sensei is a samurai of the old ways. The loser must die. Accepting defeat, the Dragon Master folds his arms across his chest and closes his eyes. I expect him to scream or beg for mercy, but he doesn't. The Dragon Master is a samurai. In the end, he knows how to die.

"Some old ways need to change." Sensei throws his staff down. "Words are not important enough to demand a life."

The crowd sighs with relief. The Dragon Master has few friends, but no one wishes him dead. Baskets bobbing, the Komusu nod approval. Words have no value to priests who rarely speak. Sensei's wisdom, like their own, is beyond words.

The Dragon Master opens his eyes. I've seen that look before. In the eyes of Black Tusk, the wild boar. It's hate. Pure hate.

Standing up, the Dragon Master barely bows. "You silly old fool. I would not have done the same for you. Don't expect such weakness from me next year." His words spit. No thank-you. No gratitude. Just hate.

Sensei doesn't care. He bows politely.

"I look forward to it. If the Dragon Master wishes to rub his scales in the dirt again, I will be honored to assist."

The Dragon Master sheathes his *katana* and wrenches his cape from an outstretched hand in the crowd.

"Next year I will crush you like the insect you are." With a flourish of red silk, he storms away. His students quickly follow.

Number One hands Sensei our trophy. The Komusu take their *shakuhachi* from under their basket-covered heads and begin to play. The Samurai Games have ended. We've won!

Nezume runs over and hugs Sensei. For once the old man is caught off balance. Except for Kyoko, we don't hug each other at the *ryu*. But Sensei is right as always: sometimes old ways need to change. I lead the charge to drown Sensei with our hugs. The Dragon Master couldn't knock him over, but we can. Sensei is lost under a sea of arms and legs.

When all the limbs are untangled, we sit waiting for our master to speak.

"I am very proud. You showed great honor and wisdom. You are truly a team. And next year Nezume will compete with us. But first I must ask Nezume an important question." His eyes dance. "What have you learned that you need to forget?"

"I know NOTHING." Nezume hangs his head in shame.

I grin. I've found a Zen friend.

Sensei claps his hands with pleasure. "Wonderful. You are way ahead on your lessons. It took me a year to teach my students nothing. Now we must pack and hurry home. We have much to do."

Dismayed, I look at Sensei, hoping he'll change his mind. For the first time ever, we're winners, ready to bask in our glory. We want to strut and show off, to party and stuff our faces with rice cakes. "What could be so important that we need to rush away?" I ask.

"It does not matter if you do not know where you are going, as long as you know where you have been," Sensei says.

I know where we've been, but I still I want to know what comes next.

"More practice!" Sensei yells, jumping up and waving his staff in the air. "Come. There is much to learn, and it cannot wait. I am a good teacher, but I am not a wizard or a magician. I cannot work miracles."

I look around at my friends' proud smiling faces and the trophy Mikko clutches tight against his chest. I remember the day we came to the *ryu*. Armless, legless, sightless, sad, and different. We're not like that anymore. We're Dragon slayers. Sensei can't fool me. He's a wizard, all right. And a magician, too. I know a miracle when I see one.

THE SEVEN VIRTUES OF BUSHIDO

義	GI	rectitude
勇	YU	courage
仁	JIN	benevolence
礼	REI	respect
真	MĀKOTO	honesty
名誉	MEIYO	honor
忠誠	CHUSEI	loyalty

USEFUL WORDS

BUSHIDO — the samurai code

CHI, JIN, YU — wisdom, benevolence, and courage — these principles form the basis of Bushido

GEMBUKU — the ceremony marking a samurai boy's coming of age

GOKIBURI — cockroach

KANJI — writing pictograph, symbol

KATANA — long curved sword, traditional weapon of the samurai

RYU — school

RYUJIN — dragon

SENSEI — teacher

SHAKUHACHI — bamboo flute played by the Komusu priests

WAKIZASHI — short pointed dagger, traditional weapon of the samurai

ACKNOWLEDGMENTS

To my terrific boys, Jackson and Cassidy; to my mentor and valued friend Di Bates; to my partners in writing crimes — Bill Condon, Ann Whitehead, Vicki Stanton, Mo Johnson, DC Green, and Sally Hall; to my sister, Neridah; to my first fan (and critic) Barbara Brown; to my wonderful editor Sue Whiting; and to two extraordinary high-school teachers, Robyn Sankey and Vic Playford. Thanks. You are all a part of this book.